Ever & Always

"You can do this. I want you to skate alone around the rest of the way."

"No, I'm scared."

"Trust me, Maddie. You've got to trust me. I'll be right behind you."

"What if I fall?"

"I can skate faster than you can fall," he whispered, and Maddie closed her eyes against the shiver that enveloped her body. He gave her a little push and she began to skate, dreading the moment he would let go. And of course, he did let go, hanging back to give her room to skate ahead.

The girls at the window were rapt, whispering and giggling quietly as they watched their hero skate with his new girlfriend. Even some of his teammates stopped near the locker room door to watch the arena and the attention Jack was paying to the pretty girl in the pink sweater.

Maddie could barely breathe.

God, I have to do this. Trust Jack. Don't let me fall!

Slowly, carefully, Maddie took the curve at the far end of the oval rink, concentrating on looking smooth and capable. She didn't dare wonder if Jack was still behind her, or how far away he was. She kept her eyes on the exit door. She was doing fine until the sound of an engine, a loud sound akin to that of a giant lawnmower, pervaded the rink and startled Maddie from her ice exhibition. Abruptly she turned her head in the direction of the sound, and the break in concentration disrupted her momentum, making her off-balance and wobbly.

Instantly she looked down at her skates, trying to get back into rhythm, but it was too late. She tried to remember how to drag the toe of her skate to brake, and in doing so made herself even more insecure. Terror filled her head. *Oh no, I'm going down!*

The thought did not even fully cross her mind and Jack was with her, his arms not merely grasping her waist but wrapped fully around her, the heat of his chest warming her back and shoulders. Looking forward, Maddie realized they were only a few feet away from the rink door.

They slowed to a stop, but still he held her, his lips close to her ear.

"Now, is there anything more I can do to earn your trust?" he whispered before kissing her neck briefly. He waited patiently for her to catch her breath, to calm down from her scare.

Maddie closed her eyes. Jack's show of affection was not lost on her, but she hesitated to acknowledge it for fear that she was over-reacting. Perhaps it was only in sympathy, a consolation for her pathetic performance. Taking a deep breath, she mentally forced aside the exhilarating feel of his lips against her skin. But she could not begin to slow the wild flutter in her chest.

"Just tell me, who *is* Sam Bony, and what is that awful noise?"

What They Are Saying About
Ever & Always

"A good mystery romance that keeps the reader guessing for most of the story. [Ever & Always] is rich with turmoil, and ties up all the loose ends.

"Ms. Carter had done an excellent job. It is rare to find a hero as believable as Jack, and a heroine as true to life as Maddie. Their trials are real life and their fears and anxieties something every reader can relate to. Ms. Carter's story is funny, touching, and poignant. A true pleasure from beginning to end."

--Tamara McHatton,
Rhapsody Magazine

"Maddie Tyler has no idea what she's setting in motion on the day she speaks to the man who was her first high school crush. Maddie is married, with a teenaged son, but her marriage is floundering, her heart is vulnerable, and Jack McKenzie is by all accounts a wonderful man. Maddie's husband wants a divorce, and Maddie realizes she doesn't love him. Soon she's falling in love with Jack. Her life is looking just about perfect. But life is not done with Maddie. Behind the scene, someone is watching, someone who has a vested interest in how Maddie's life turns out.

"Anne Carter writes competently about life and love. Her characters are real with flaws as well as heroic qualities. [This] is Maddie's story, and following her sometimes mundane, sometimes turbulent life, is fascinating. 4-1/2 stars"

--Rickey R. Mallory,
Affaire de Coeur

"A VERY enjoyable story, unique and thought-provoking. [EVER & ALWAYS] has so many unique and exciting twists and turns that I couldn't turn my [ereader] off until I knew how Anne

Carter planned to solve her heroine's dilemma! The characters are well-drawn and believable, the story unlike any romance I've read. It leaves the reader with a smile and the feeling that Jack McKenzie and Madelyn Cross were made for each other. I would recommend this book to anyone in search of a satisfying, warm-hearted romance."

--Kate Douglas, Award winning author of
HONEYSUCKLE ROSE
ON WINGS OF LOVE

"EVER & ALWAYS is the sweet, tear-jerking story of two people who have both failed miserably in love, but finally get it right... [Maddie and Jack's] love is of the sweetest kind, and their chemistry is wonderful."

--Christine Chambers
Romantic Times Book Club

Ever & Always

By

Anne Carter

Beacon Street Books

Contemporary Romance

Beacon Street Books

EVER & ALWAYS

by Anne Carter

A Beacon Point Romance - Prequel

Print ISBN 978-0692208267

Portions Previously Published under ISBN 1-59088-965-7
as "In Too Deep"

Published In the United States Of America

May, 2014

Beacon Street Books
Santa Clarita, CA 91355-2026
http://www.beaconstreetbooks.com

Dedication

For Mom,
who shared my love of romance
and loved everything I write,

and for Daddy,
who shared my love of writing
and encouraged me from day one,

I thank you from the bottom of my heart
for always supporting me in everything I do.

Prologue

Maddie sat on the edge of the bed. Groggy, she stared at the clock radio on the nightstand, uncomprehending at first: how did it get so late? She knew she was run-down, but had not expected the fifteen-minute rest to become a three-hour nap.

"Better start dinner," she murmured. Alone in the house, she spoke to no one but herself, slowly getting to her feet and pausing to rub her eyes. "Man, I am tired."

No good reason for it. What had she done today? A little gardening. Paid her parents a visit. Balanced her checkbook. Folded some towels.

Pausing in front of her dresser, she brushed her hair, tangled from her midday nap. And no wonder, she thought, grimacing as she forced the brush through her waist-long tresses. Leaning close to the mirror, Maddie frowned at the dark circles beneath her eyes. Weren't you supposed to look rested after a nap?

She slid her bare feet into a pair of worn fuzzy slippers and shuffled off toward the kitchen, trying to remember what she had planned to cook and also what it was that had awakened her.

"Stuffed peppers. It was definitely stuffed peppers." She closed the refrigerator door and smirked to herself. Thomas loved bell peppers. The thought of him kick-started her memory; it was his phone call that had jarred her awake.

"The storm will be in by dinnertime. I'm going down to the slip and make sure the boat is secure," he had told her.

"What did the doctor say?" Maddie had asked. Now, gathering together her recipe items, she struggled to remember his response.

"Getting better," or something like that. The doctor was encouraged; the cancer hadn't spread.

"Yes." Maddie nodded while running cold water over the green bells. "It was good news." She smiled, staring out the kitchen window that looked over the vegetable garden. Nearly dusk, the sky was deceptively darker due to the gathering rain clouds above the canyon. It was clearly a big storm, and Thomas had been right to worry about his sailboat in the marina.

Maddie prepared a sumptuous meal. Wine-soaked Portobello mushrooms for appetizers, a variation on a Caesar's salad, and a hot beef consommé to ward off the chill. The stuffed peppers were beautifully arrayed on a platter. Candles rising from a centerpiece of local greenery graced the dining room table. In the refrigerator was a chocolate cheesecake.

The storm broke overhead at around 7:30 p.m., and Maddie was already pacing the floor. It was unusual for Thomas to be so late without calling. Highly unusual. At eight o'clock she tried calling the small office on the boat dock near their slip but got no answer. Trying to remain calm, she finally covered the meal and slipped the plates into the refrigerator, unable to take even one bite.

Outside, the wind shrieked through the canyon, and Maddie imagined it clawing ruthlessly through her garden, uprooting the tender plants and dragging them away. An intermittent tapping on the front window sent her running to peer through the glass at the small hailstones pummeling the panes. In the distance she could see the unmistakable brilliance of lightning offshore.

In the kitchen was a small television. Maddie furiously and repetitively pressed the remote's "on" button; getting the controller repaired had not been a priority. Now, at last, the screen came to life and Maddie hurriedly scanned the stations in search of storm-related news.

"They're calling it a squall," the weather guy was saying, his pointer indicating an area just outside the L.A. harbor. "Most unusual and posing a real threat to any vessel not safely moored by now. The Coast Guard is recommending anyone with knowledge of a non-returning craft to advise them immediately."

Maddie sank slowly into a kitchen chair. Thomas was not out today; he had plainly stated his intentions—to tie the boat down. Unless he was helping someone else…yes, it was possible. Her man had a generous heart when it came to aiding others in need. Perhaps that's where he was.

He'd be calling any minute.

One

"I wonder if we'll see any stars," Todd said as he and his mother hurried across the NBC Studios guest parking lot toward the lobby doors. Humoring him, she shrugged a "maybe" kind of shrug, not wanting to dash his childish hopes of possibly bumping into one of his TV heroes. And for just a brief moment, she shared some of that magical anticipation; who's to say one of these cars didn't belong to Ashton Kutcher or James Spader?

"Whatcha gonna do while I'm in there?" Todd wanted to know as they reached the entrance. "Read one of your *law* books?" He opened his mouth wide and pretended to stick his finger into his throat.

"Nope. Today I'm treating myself to a romance. None of your business anyway," she said, wrinkling her nose comically. "See you later."

Maddie Tyler gave her son a discreet wave and left him waiting with the others in the lobby. The park across the street seemed as good a place as any to pass the time until Todd was finished, so she found a bench with an adequate view of the studio doors and opened a book.

The morning air felt crisp but not particularly cold, the sun burning off all but the last traces of last night's cloud cover. She couldn't seem to stay with the book; the people in the park were more fun to watch. Behind her, boys kicked around a soccer ball, their shouts of both triumph and disappointment carried on the breeze in sporadic puffs. A couple sitting beneath a tree reminded her that indeed, the world could end any day, and they were making the best of it. Maddie sighed, remembering when it really didn't matter if the grass was damp.

There were the usual Frisbee-catching dogs and skateboarders grinding along the curbs. Somewhere the rhythmic *plat! plat! plat!* of a basketball dribbled along an asphalt court. Young mommies pushed tots in swings and all seemed just right with the world.

Across the street, cars came and went from the NBC parking lot. Maddie remembered that as a teen, she was in awe of even riding past a real studio. Surely every car belonged to a star, driven by the likes of Matt Damon, Brad Pitt or Ben Affleck.

She was startled from her daydream by an abrupt *thump!* against the back of the bench. She retrieved the errant soccer ball and tossed it back to the waiting goaltender. The breeze felt wonderful. On a whim, she pulled the barrette from her hair and shook it out with her fingers. These days she didn't care too much about how it looked; without the patience to either straighten or curl it, she'd taken to wearing a bun wound up in a large clip.

Turning back toward the street, she noticed a man pushing a baby stroller down the sidewalk. What a great sight, a dad taking time out to walk his child on this beautiful day! As she watched them proceed up the street, she noticed something small and yellow fall from the stroller. The man kept on walking.

She waited a few seconds to see if he noticed the object, then tossed her book onto the bench and gave chase after the man and stroller, now far down the block. The lost item turned out to be a small knitted bootie, which she picked up, and she walked quickly behind the man. She had almost caught up with them when the man turned unexpectedly, nearly running her down with the stroller.

"Oh!" she said in surprise, bending down to brush off the toe of her shoe.

"I'm sorry," he said, pushing the stroller to the side. "Are you all right?"

"I'm fine, but you dropped this back there, and I didn't think you were coming back," she offered, rising to hand over the yellow bootie. Looking into his face for the first time Maddie was stunned; this was a face she knew all too well. Unfortunately, it was obvious he did not remember hers.

"Oh, man, thanks a lot. His mom would have pitched a fit. I didn't even notice it was gone."

"Well, that stuff happens…a bootie, a bottle, a pacifier…babies are always losing things." Feeling awkward, Maddie began walking slowly backwards in the general direction of her bench.

"You must have kids," he said, squatting down to slip the missing bootie onto the baby's bare foot.

"Oh, yeah. Yes indeed. Just one."

"Maybe you could help me then," he said, a confused frown creasing his face as he bent over the boy. He carefully tugged open the tiny sweater to show her something beneath. Returning, Maddie peered into the stroller beside this not-so-strange stranger.

"Have I gotten this all screwed up or what?" he asked, pointing to the snaps on the baby's undershirt. He took another moment to count the snaps, pointing out that there was an extra one at the bottom. Maddie took that moment to gaze at his face.

The years had been kind to him. His light brown hair

still shone gold in the sun. It no longer brushed his shoulders, but was still thick. Maddie couldn't help but notice how it curled over his collar and fell rakishly just above his brow. His face was a little more lined, not quite as full.

Still handsome, charming and fit. Of course.

He turned to her and she felt fluid and warm under his gaze, his brown eyes waiting for a response. A simple, honest look, yet she was mesmerized.

"Well, it's not exactly right." Maddie began to giggle, feeling giddy, silly, embarrassed by her own thoughts. "But don't worry. He's none the worse for it. I do believe he needs a change, though," she said, straightening up.

The un-stranger sighed and stood. "I'm terrible at this stuff. I was hoping his mother would get back before I had to, uh, you know, get into diapers and such…again."

Was he always this tall?

The silence turned awkward. Maddie looked back at the cooing child and her heart warmed. It had been over ten years since she'd held an infant. She cleared her throat.

"I can help you if you'd like. Roll him up to that bench. What's his name, anyway?"

"Duncan. She—his mother—had an appointment in there." He motioned across the street. "So we're hanging out for an hour or so."

"How old is he? 'Bout six months?"

"Almost. Next week, I think." He lifted Duncan from the stroller and Maddie grabbed the quilt he'd been lying on and spread it on the bench. The baby made a noise, a kind of grunting sound that babies always make, and his father began to bounce him up and down the way fathers always do. They were all the same, no matter who they were.

She tugged a diaper bag from the stroller's basket and boldly started pawing through it. She already knew, of course, what would be inside, and quickly located a diaper and a package of travel baby wipes. Duncan began to cry and fuss the moment he was placed on the bench. She changed him quickly and efficiently. After all, she had changed hundreds of diapers in her life.

"Wow. You're good," her almost-friend said, shaking his head.

Without a thought, she picked up the complaining child and put him to her shoulder. He stopped crying and lay down his head.

With nothing to say, they both glanced across the street. He spoke first.

"I'm sorry, I'm keeping you from something."

"No, I'm just waiting for my son. He won't be out for fifteen minutes or so."

"Is he auditioning?"

"He's in a focus group. They rate new TV shows for kids. He's eleven," she explained.

"Ah." A brief pause.

She unconsciously rocked back and forth, and although she couldn't see his face, she knew Duncan was drifting off to Baby La-La. "Little sweetie," she murmured, briefly closing her eyes and breathing in the baby's mother-intoxicating scent.

"Excuse me?"

"Your son. He's adorable."

"Thanks." Her companion smiled and ran his fingers through his hair. "Mind if I sit down? I played hockey last night and my legs are beat."

Still playing hockey!

Maddie wrapped the quilt around the sleeping child and gently settled him back in his stroller.

"Now, if I had done that, he'd be wailing already," his

father marveled, leaning close to the baby and lightly tucking the quilt in. "My parenting skills are not quite what they should be."

Maddie smiled and joined him on the bench.

"I guess I should explain. We're separated, and my time with him is…limited," he said suddenly.

I know. It was in last week's People *Magazine.* "I'm sorry. It's, uh, tough these days."

"Well…at the risk of *sounding* cliché, I guess we *were* kind of cliché. We just rushed things. Plus, she's in her twenties, just starting an acting career, and I'm-well, pushing forty…"

No you're not. You'll be 37 in May.

"You married?"

"Yes." Maddie answered, looking away at nothing in particular.

"Overall, I've been mostly single. I think when you're alone that long, it's hard to adapt to someone being with you all the time."

She nodded. What else could she do? Tell him he was an idiot for hooking up with a younger woman? *Hardly! His history couldn't begin to compare with mine.*

"Sometimes I think it's just not in the cards," he murmured, and looked down at the grass.

"Maybe you're using the wrong deck."

He looked up then, and she sensed he was looking for meaning to her words. Warily, she continued. "Perhaps…you're an unconventional person, looking for an unconventional relationship." Maddie imparted her words of wisdom, feeling both expert and ridiculous at the same time. Besides, she knew she'd never see him again, so what did it matter what she said? It had been a long, long time since she'd dreamed of being his perfect woman.

"Unconventional. That's a new one." He grinned at her then, showing dimples she was thrilled to see. "I guess you could say that."

"I meant no disrespect," she said, smiling back. "I'm just saying that long-term marriages, full-on lifetime commitments aren't for everybody. Sometimes, some *people*, just need a *sometimes* partner." She was getting in deep here. "I think."

"Hmmm."

Maddie's head began to spin. She wished someone would come along, slap her face and wake her up! She feared she might jump into his lap at any moment. Unable to stop, she plunged on.

"I mean, just because it works for some people, doesn't mean there's something wrong with *you*, you know? You have the right to look for something that works for *you*." She paused, clearing her throat. "So. That's my unsolicited, somewhat biased, overstated opinion. I'll shut up now."

"Biased?"

"Never mind." *Somebody stop me!*

"Well, I appreciate your sharing your thoughts." He looked at the stroller, then back to her. "And, as a matter of fact, I appreciate that you even took the time to stop and help me. Do you realize people just don't do that stuff anymore? Nobody wants to get involved."

"I think people are basically afraid of strangers," she said, which was safe because he didn't really know he was not a stranger to her.

In her head, the son-checking alarm went off and Maddie looked across the street just in time to see half a dozen kids exiting the glass doors, each presumably with a crisp $20 bill in hand. She stood up. Todd would soon be heading this way.

“Well, I wish you luck.” She began to edge away, hoping her reluctance to go wasn’t too obvious. Then, lamely, she iced the cake. “Don’t be so hard on yourself. I’m sure you tried. Someone good will happen to you—I mean, some*thing*, Jeez!” She laughed, almost stumbling as she performed her walking-backwards-on-the-grass trick again.

He nodded, bestowing those dimples upon her once more. She thought she would expire under his gaze. When she reached the sidewalk, she called back to him.

“It was great seeing you again, Jack! You are even more charming than you were in high school!”

Now he laughed out loud in surprise. He even *sounded* better than she remembered.

He stood by the bench and waved to her, calling out as she stepped into the street. “Hey! Will you be here next Saturday?”

Two

Conversation was sparse at the dinner table. Maddie looked from her husband to her son, both preoccupied while eating.

"So, what kind of show did you see today?" Ray Tyler finally asked, breaking the silence.

"It was another one of those 'after-school skate club type shows'," Maddie answered.

"How was it, Todd?" Ray asked, looking directly at Maddie.

"It was dumb," Todd spoke up.

"If it's so dumb, why do you go?" Ray wanted to know, although his tone belied the fact that he really didn't care.

"Hey, it's twenty bucks..." Todd murmured.

Ray nodded, and it was clear the conversation was over. After several minutes, Ray spoke again.

"I forgot to tell you. *Mountaineer* is sending me back to Colorado next week."

Maddie nodded. So that's what was bugging Ray. He knew she'd be disappointed, and probably dreaded telling her the news. She forced a smile. "Well. Glad to know they're choosing you over Ted Starling."

"Yeah, well, Ted's being in Chile could have something to do with it."

Ray took his plate to the sink, and then left the room. Maddie was afraid to look at Todd, afraid to expose him to the sadness in her eyes. Instead, she spoke brightly, "Let's get started on that homework, 'kay?"

Todd helped her clear the table and even put some of the dishes into the dishwasher before retrieving his books. Maddie looked after him with affection.

That evening Ray asked about her week.

"We're pretty busy at work. A new partner is joining the firm, and he doesn't have a secretary yet. Even the paralegals are helping us to get the guy organized."

Obviously bored with her news, Ray nodded and began flipping the TV stations with the remote. The 52" screen was really too big for their family room, but Ray had insisted on buying it and Maddie couldn't really complain. He made good money climbing rocks for a living. Slight but agile, Ray Tyler was considered one of the best "mountain men" in the country and had conquered most of the world's highest and most treacherous peaks.

She looked at her husband of so many years and wondered; who was he? Or more to the point, who were *they*? Maddie scanned her memory for a picture of Ray. Perhaps on their honeymoon, when they had rafted on the Kern River. Had she been scared? No, only *petrified.* Ray had seduced her into going, seduced her with his laughing blue eyes, challenging her, maybe even blackmailing her a little. His lithe, sinewy body was gleaming wet in the sun, his white teeth flashing that rogue smile, his blue-black hair dripping onto his brow. He pulled hard on the oars, seemingly unconcerned with her ineptitude at keeping up, unconcerned with her fear. Danger enticed him. Aroused him.

She recalled, with a shiver, the times they skied at Vail.

He persuaded, no, demanded, that she begin with the intermediates rather than the beginners. She could do it, he insisted, and was impatient for her to join him on the bigger slopes. But the smile never left his face. It was the excitement, the thrill that kept it there. Which was, she now realized with regret, why it no longer graced his attractive face. As much as she hated clichés, she had to accept that, for Ray at least, the thrill was gone.

Maddie twisted her wedding ring, ruefully remembering that Ray never wore one. He didn't wear any jewelry at all.

In the beginning, they had done everything together. Trips, adventures, parties. The Rockies, Sierras and the Andes. But Maddie had tired of dragging a small child to the coldest spots on earth, and when Todd began public schooling, Maddie tossed out the anchor. At first, Ray didn't seem to mind her missing a trip here and there, whimpering like a lost puppy at his supposed loneliness. But soon, the humor faded and Ray began to withdraw, telling her less and less about his escapades, and spending more of his home time focused on the television. Tonight was no different.

His channel surfing made her nervous, but Maddie kept her impatience in check. It seemed like Ray was home so little, she wanted to spend as much time with him as she could.

"Would you like some wine?" she asked, ready to rise from the couch.

"Nope." Ray glanced at her casually. "Have some, if you want."

"No, I don't want any." Maddie folded her hands in her lap. Her thoughts turned back to her day. She had not mentioned to Ray her chance meeting with Jack McKenzie in the park.

Jack. How long had it been? She was a sophomore at Delaney High School. Jack was a senior, and while he wasn't the most popular or even the best looking, Madelyn Cross had been attracted to the varsity hockey star. It helped that Jack never seemed to be attached to any one girl. But try as she might to throw herself in his path, Jack McKenzie graduated without so much as a wink in her direction.

"What are you smiling about?" Ray asked.

"Oh, nothing. Just thinking about something that happened when I was in high school."

He didn't ask her to elaborate.

It was Tuesday afternoon when the call came from Gladys at NBC; they wanted Todd back for another screening, on Saturday, could he make it?

"I don't see why not. If there's money in it, he'll be there," Maddie replied with a laugh. She was anxious to tell Todd when he got home.

The rest of the week passed uneventfully and Saturday morning found Maddie again driving Todd to the studios. The skies were gray, heavy with unspent rain, and Maddie debated about sitting in the park. At home, Ray was checking his equipment and beginning to pack. It was one place she just didn't want to be. The day wasn't particularly cold, just gloomy, so she decided to risk it. She could run for the car if it started to rain. And maybe this time she'd get past the prologue of her book.

Today, the park was empty except for an old man walking an even older dog. The noise of the traffic on the boulevard seemed louder than before. Wrapping her sweater tighter, she sat on the bench and tried to concentrate on the novel.

She had almost bought into the story when she

suddenly felt she was no longer alone. Looking up, she was startled to see Jack McKenzie walking toward her from the street.

"So, you *are* here again," he said with a smile.

"Well, yeah, but I don't know for how long," she replied, looking up at the sky. Inside, she felt a hum, a pleasant sense of well-being. She realized with surprise that she was thrilled to see Jack. He looked more casual today, in jeans and a white T-shirt under a black leather jacket. He seemed relaxed, confident, and happy to see her, too.

Almost on cue, sporadic raindrops began to fall.

"What brings you back here?" she asked, slipping her book inside her sweater.

"Nothing. I was driving past on my way home and I saw you sitting here. Just thought I'd stop and say hello."

Maddie stared at Jack a moment too long. *Just thought he'd stop?* Fortunately, her growing anxiety was sidetracked by heavier rain.

"How long do you have?" Jack asked, gesturing toward the studio with his head.

"He just went in. They said an hour."

"Then you have time for coffee."

"Oh, I don't know…"

The rain was insistent; so was Jack. "C'mon. It's right across the street. Warm and dry."

Well, it was coffee with Jack or an hour sitting in her car; an easy decision. Dodging traffic and raindrops, they raced across the boulevard and were seated in no time.

Maddie's breathless laughter surprised her. She was already glad she'd accepted Jack's offer, and he rewarded her with a warm smile.

"So, when did you know it was me?" he asked, signaling the waitress for two coffees.

"Oh, just about the time you crippled me with your stroller."

"Ah." He nodded. "I'm good at that. Just ask my dog."

"I can walk fine now, thank you." Maddie reached for the cream. "How's little Duncan?"

"Haven't seen him."

"Oh." Maddie nodded knowingly. "I see. Well then, how's your dog?"

"Dog? What dog?"

"The one you flattened with the stroller."

Jack grinned in appreciation of her quick wit, then assumed a casual pose. "So, what have you been doing the last twenty years, Madelyn Cross?"

Maddie nearly dropped the creamer at Jack's words. Coloring, she looked away briefly. *He did remember me!*

When she didn't speak, he continued.

"I admit, I didn't recognize you at first. I wasn't sure, and I didn't want to embarrass myself, I'd already done that." He shrugged and took a sip of coffee. "Let's have breakfast."

Against her mild protestations, Jack ordered a full breakfast for each of them. And as he talked about a million different things, Maddie found herself fascinated by his easy manner and friendly nature.

"I remember one time in particular," he was saying between bites, "in the library. You asked me to help you find a book. I could never figure out why, when you already had the book in the stack under your backpack. I saw it there later." He shook his head comically.

"Couldn't figure it out, huh?" Maddie asked with a grin. "Typical."

"Typical? What's that supposed to mean?"

"You were being a typical, bone-headed jock."

Jack opened his eyes wide in mock surprise.

"You…wanted me to notice you?"

Now Maddie blushed. "Of course."

Jack loaded his toast with egg and stuffed it in his mouth, nodding. After swallowing and taking another sip of coffee, he showed her his dimples. "You were too young for me. And anyway, you never came to any of my games."

"My father wouldn't let me." She pouted, lowering her eyes. "He thought hockey was evil. And the fact that the rink was off-campus didn't help. I finally decided I would hit on you at graduation, and you didn't show up! Do you know how hard it was to convince my parents that I had to be there? And your buddies had the nerve to lie for you and say you were in the hospital of all things!" The frustration of her broken teenaged heart came pouring out.

"Mmm. I was." Jack said casually. "Pass the jelly?"

"*What?*"

"True. Broke both my arms the night before on the ice."

"No! Then how come I didn't know about it?" Maddie demanded.

Jack chuckled. "Well, apparently you did. You just didn't want to believe it. We hushed it up because, well, we weren't supposed to be on the rink that night." He shook his head at the memory.

"So, I've been mad at you for twenty years for nothing?" Maddie asked.

Jack leaned across the table, his expression serious. "You forgive me?"

Maddie pretended to weigh his excuse. Finally she gave him a questioning, if cynical, look. "Are you buying breakfast?"

"You bet."

"Okay then." She nodded definitively and then broke

into a giggle.

"So what did you do after you gave up on me? Let's see; you got hitched right out of high school, had a bunch of kids and you drive a minivan."

"I *was* barely out of high school when I fell in love and ran off with the man of my dreams, yeah. One child, and I drive an F150 truck. I'm a researcher for a law firm downtown, I'm married to a climber, and my son, Todd, is the best thing that ever happened to me."

"Wow…a climber did you say? As in, ladder? Social? Corporate?"

"As in *mountain*."

Jack nodded, frowning. "Okay," he said. "Mountain."

Maddie laughed. "That's how most people react. Ray's a top-class rock climber. He's been all over the world, he has sponsors, he does commercials…" Her voice trailed away as she was reminded of the fact that her husband was leaving again.

"That keeps life interesting, I bet. Does Todd climb, too?"

"Oh, no. He has no interest in it. Oh, he likes to go hiking, sometimes he and I go out to the local hills and hike around, but he never goes with Ray." Fearing she'd say too much, Maddie looked for a change in subject. "How about you. You went on to college, right?"

"British Columbia U. A hockey scholarship. I studied art for a couple of years until it got boring. Then I joined the Air Force, then the Forestry Department. Drew maps, field guides, you know." Jack rattled on, looking into her eyes. "Then after that I became a transvestite and went on to Broadway…"

Maddie giggled again. Clearly, Jack enjoyed making her laugh, and she adored the attention. She found herself wanting to know everything about him. "What do you do now?"

"I'm a designer. I design movie sets, television sets, and lately I've done a couple of concerts. It's fun, it's flexible, and it gives me lots of time to think…about what I want to do next."

The time flew by. Jack delighted her with tales about the various shows he'd worked on and the finicky rock band for whom he'd just completed a set. And too soon, he was pointing to his watch.

The rain had stopped, leaving a musty, close feeling to the air outside. Jack walked Maddie to the studio entrance where they waited for Todd.

Standing beside Jack, Maddie noticed his tall, athletic build. *He must be taller than Ray by four or five inches.*

"Penny for your thoughts?" he asked, interrupting her daydream.

"Oh, nothing. But I do want to thank you again for breakfast, and for the conversation. You brought back a lot of fond memories."

"Same here, Maddie."

Todd was the first to swing open the heavy glass doors.

"How was it?" Maddie asked.

Todd looked hesitant, glancing at his mother's companion and back to her.

"You can tell the truth. Jack's a friend," she said with a smile.

"It sucked, Mom, big time. I don't know where they get those ideas. They act like we're still in kindergarten."

"Too bad. By the way, Todd, this is Jack McKenzie. We went to high school together."

Todd nodded a hello.

"Jack works here sometimes."

"Yeah, I was just about to tell your mom, anytime you want to come down and tour some of the sets, I'd be glad to show you around."

"The sets? Really? That'd be really cool. Can we, Mom?" Todd's spirits increased tenfold. "Wow. Are you a director or something?"

"Naw. I just design the sets. They tell me what the show is about, what kind of scenes it has, and I make up an idea for a set. Sometimes I build the models, too."

"Way cool. Can we, Mom?" Todd asked again.

Maddie just smiled.

"Sure, why don't you all come? Bring your dad, too. We'll get lunch at the commissary." Clearly, Jack had decided. Maddie nodded and Jack handed her a card. "Call me."

So. Sweet little Madelyn Cross had grown up. Jack started his car and turned on the wipers; the rain had returned. *What a nice girl. Woman*, he reminded himself. The reminiscing had sent him back. Too bad she was married. To a rock climber yet!

At home, he started the teakettle and went on to his bedroom. On the closet floor was a trunk containing the only things in the townhouse that were personal to him. His past.

Dragging the trunk out into the room, he threw open the heavy lid and lifted out several miscellaneous items, none of which were his target today. Finally, near the bottom, he slipped his fingers underneath a book, a heavily bound album and pulled it to the surface. Emblazoned across the cover in ornate raised letters were the words "Delaney High School." In the lower right corner, pressed in gold, was the name "Ian Arthur McKenzie."

Smiling to himself, Jack took the yearbook and went

back to the kitchen to make a cup of instant coffee. Quickly turning to the section titled "Sophomores," he scanned the photos for the one of the young girl with the huge crush on the shy hockey star.

Three

"It's just for a couple of hours, Ray. We thought Friday afternoon would be good, since it's a school holiday."

"Madelyn, you know I go to the gym on Fridays. I really have to be in shape for this climb. I'm leaving Monday, you know." Ray had maps spread across the kitchen table and was carefully plotting his next adventure.

Maddie sighed audibly. She wasn't above letting Ray know he disappointed her. Todd was so looking forward to the studio tour Jack had offered, and she thought this would be a great family activity. She wanted Ray to meet Jack; she wasn't sure why.

"It's just that we never do anything together anymore. Remember when Todd was little and we used to go on picnics, we took him to the zoo, Sea World, places like that? I miss that, Ray. It seems like we just coexist here."

Ray put his pen down and approached Maddie, wrapping his arms around her. He kissed her cheek, then her ear. "You're right. We do need to get out more. And I promise, next time, next time an opportunity comes up, I'll go."

He rubbed her back affectionately, and Maddie closed her eyes. She wished she could believe him. Slipping her fingers around the back of his neck, she longed to run them through his shining jet hair, only to be reminded with dismay that Ray had recently cropped his hair short.

Opening her eyes, Maddie leaned away from Ray, peering into his for some sign of truth.

He smiled. "What?"

"You really can't go with us?"

Ray's smile faded and he released her. "I guess you really don't care how important this climb is to me."

"It's not that, Ray. It just seems like a small effort on your part. Just—never mind. And, by the way, open house at Todd's school is next week. I guess I'll just go by myself, again."

Maddie left the room. Ray went back to his maps.

"Do we still get to go?" Todd wanted to know as he watched his mother put away his clean laundry. "Even if he doesn't?"

"Well, I've thought about it," Maddie said, now sitting on the bed. "And I've decided, yes, darn it. We'll go and have a good time. And if Jack wants to take us to lunch, we'll do that, too."

Todd laughed and hugged his mother.

It was after midnight when Ray finally joined her in bed. She hadn't been able to sleep, and was tossing as he slid in beside her. Soon, he reached for her and she tiredly slipped into his arms.

"I'm sorry, Maddie. I really am. I haven't been much good lately. It's kind of like a fever. I feel like I've got to be climbing all the time. I'm miserable when I'm waiting." He laid his head on her chest, and she hugged him, although she had no answer.

"Maybe after Colorado, things will settle down a bit. I should really take some time off. You, me and Todd, maybe we'll take a vacation or two. We could go back to San Diego, hell, we could go to Italy if you want."

Italy? Where did that come from? Has he already forgotten how much I want to visit France?

"You're still special to me, Maddie. I wish you would come with me to Colorado. I know, I know, you can't, but I still wish you could." Ray whispered in the dark against her breast. "Elise is going. You two could have fun while I'm on the mountain…"

"Elise is a lot of fun. I do wish I could, Ray. But it just wouldn't work out right now. I can't take the time off work, and Todd's soccer tryouts are next week, and open house…"

Ray sighed, then began kissing the warm hollow of her neck in an obvious attempt to arouse her. While she didn't particularly feel like having sex, Maddie tried to respond to his efforts. Her craving for intimacy was strong, despite the fact that their lovemaking had long since stopped resembling anything akin to *making love*. Tonight, she was willing to settle. And she hated herself for doing it.

They left the house at noon on Friday, Todd chattering excitedly and Maddie a nervous wreck. She made two wrong turns on the way and drove in the "out" driveway at the studio, prompting a shaking fist or two from other drivers. When at last they parked, she made a cursory glance in the visor mirror. *I guess I look all right.*

"Mom, c'mon!" Todd admonished, already out of the car and opening her door.

Jack waited at the entrance, chatting amicably with the guard on duty. "Hey, there!" he called, and then greeted Todd with a handshake, a gesture that made Todd visibly taller and instantly more reserved. Maddie exchanged a smile with Jack, who then took her hand in both of his.

"So glad you guys came down. Sorry to hear Ralph couldn't make it."

"Ray," Maddie said softly.

"Right. Well, my friends, right this way."

As they walked their way through sit-coms, hospital dramas and talk shows, Jack explained the "back side" of each set, pointing out what was real and what was artificial or facade. He showed them plans and sketches, detailing how each set begins as an illustration. Todd was beside himself over his good fortune, storing up the data to relate to his friends at school.

The tour ended at the studio commissary.

"Anything you like," Jack said, marveling at how big Todd's eyes got as he perused the dessert counter in the cafeteria. "Just get a tray and load it up, pal."

"I might suggest a sandwich first, TJ," Maddie put in, earning her a bonafide eye-roll.

They dined companionably. As others came and went, Jack pointed out a celebrity, a director and one of the network executives. Todd was speechless.

"So, what are you into, Todd? Do you like school?"

"School's okay. I mostly like to do experiments. I have a rocket collection, but I haven't done too much with it yet 'cuz Ray has to help me and, well, he isn't around much lately. Mom won't let me do it by myself."

Maddie cringed inwardly. Todd's reference to "Ray" stung and the comment about her restriction made her feel overprotective. Jack, however, didn't miss a beat.

"Ah. She's right about that. So what sports do you like? Baseball? Football? Swimming?"

"Well, I kinda like baseball. I play soccer with Parks and Rec. But I love hockey the most of all."

Jack's eyebrows shot up. "Yeah?" He turned to Maddie, his eyes suspicious. "You prime him?"

"Nope." She shrugged and looked back at her son.

"Well I'm pretty fond of hockey myself. Ever play?"

"Last summer I played roller hockey in the street, but someday I wanna try ice."

"How about the NHL? Ever go to any Kings or Ducks games?"

"No, Sir." Todd shrugged. "I'd sure like to go. The Kings are *bad*."

"He means *good*, of course," Maddie explained.

Jack again looked at Maddie, then shifted in his seat and cleared his throat.

"Well, you ought to get on to that dad of yours, tell him to get off his butt and take you. It's great fun." This, surely, was a crime, Jack's eyes now conveyed.

Maddie sighed to herself. She wished Jack hadn't said it, but at the same time she was angry with Ray all over again. Jack seemed so genuinely interested in Todd, and truly regretful that Todd had not seen his favorite team play.

They said their good-byes in the parking lot.

"Nice truck," Jack teased as Maddie climbed into the cab of her Ford. "Sure beats a minivan."

"Thanks for everything, Jack."

"My pleasure. Hey, I meant to ask you, that law firm you work for, was it Dewey, Cheatum and Howe?"

Maddie laughed. "Adams and Stern."

"Oh. Just in case I ever need legal representation. You understand."

"Of course. Take care, Jack."

He gave her a little salute and walked back toward the studio.

Ray was on the phone when they got home. And when he later asked about their afternoon, Maddie responded with a simple, "It was fun." Somehow, it didn't seem right to share their enjoyment with Ray.

The weekend passed with Maddie moving through a fog of discontent. While Ray went about the business of preparing for his trip and Todd spent time with his friends, Maddie felt alienated and withdrawn. She couldn't account for her mood, hoping it would soon pass.

Monday morning she told Ray good-bye. He would leave while she was at work, and her emotions were mixed. She had to admit to herself that she was partly glad to see him go. Lately, she walked on eggshells around him, always wanting something from him, something he obviously wasn't prepared to give. And it seemed to have accelerated lately. What had changed?

Her blue demeanor spilled into Tuesday, and by Wednesday morning her co-workers were ready to commit her. So it was with little enthusiasm that she answered the office phone, until Wednesday afternoon when the caller's voice jump-started her heart.

"Hi, it's Jack."

Prepared to take still another message for Paul, her boss, the sound of Jack's voice caused her pencil lead to snap completely off.

"Hi," she said softly, glancing around to see if anyone witnessed her blush. "What can I do for you?"

"Well, I was just wondering. I have these tickets lying around, season tickets, good seats, and I thought maybe Ral-*Ray* might want to take Todd."

"Tickets?"

"I'm sorry. Los Angeles Kings tickets. Rink-side at

Staples."

"Gee, when?" Maddie looked down. Her hands were quivering.

"Um…well, these are for Friday night, or I have Saturday, and some others but they're on school nights, which I assume is a no-no."

Maddie bit her lip. How could she explain to Jack that Ray was a terrible father? That Ray put himself before Todd, before herself?

"Gosh, I'm sorry. Ray's out of town for the whole week, maybe ten days."

"Man. That's too bad. These are good games too. It's a shame he's never been. I keep thinking about that." Jack paused. "Well, you know, *you* could take him."

"*Me*? Oh, no, I don't think so. I-I, I wouldn't be that much fun. I'm not up on the game or anything."

"Too bad. Unless…"

"What?"

"Would you mind if I took him?"

Maddie brought her fingernails to her teeth, and then chastised herself silently. "You don't have to do that."

"I know. But I'd like to, if you'll let me. I can pick him up, say, 5:00 on Friday night? Just give me directions to your house."

"But …"

"I'll take good care of him, I promise. You know, Maddie, it'll be a long time before I can take Duncan to a game. When I talk to Todd, my fatherly instincts kick in."

She could almost see his smile, his warm eyes, and his small joke touched her heart. "What can I possibly say to that? I can't wait to tell him. What should he bring?"

"Oh, maybe just a small camera. I might be able to introduce him to a couple of the guys."

Maddie covered her mouth for an instant with her hand, hoping to keep herself from screaming in the office. She could already feel Todd's excitement.

"You are a sweetheart," she said without thinking, then clapped her hand over her mouth again.

"I know."

She couldn't wait to tell Todd. At home, Todd was building a peanut butter and banana sandwich when Maddie walked in. "How was school?" she asked while glancing through the mail.

"Okay," Todd replied. He licked his fingers and reached for his backpack, which lay on the floor near the kitchen door. He pulled out a sheet of paper. "I'm supposed to give this to you."

"What is it?" Maddie took the paper and perused it. "Some kind of credit report?"

"We're doing this thing about identity theft. You signed a form a week ago saying it was all right to do. But that paper has some stuff on it I don't understand."

Maddie lowered herself into a chair. Here was sensitive information about Todd: his birth date, social security number, home address. Near the middle, a section was labeled "assets," and below that, an account with City Trust Bank. "There must be some mistake. You don't have an account at this bank. You don't have a bank account at all."

"That's what I told the counselor at school. She said to give it to you."

"Hmm." Maddie frowned and read the paper again. Clearly, a bank account had been opened in Todd's name. "Tuition savings fund," she read from the bottom of the page. Below that was printed, "Madelyn Tyler, as trustee for Todd Joseph La Forge." The balance was $40,000.00.

"Couldn't be Ray."

"Ray? No, pretty sure not."

"He never gives me anything except maybe five dollars sometimes."

Maddie pondered; forty thousand dollars? It had to be a mistake. She put the statement in her purse for now. "So, Jack called today. He's got a problem you might be able to help with."

"Yeah? What?"

"Apparently, he needs someone... to go with him to a Kings game."

Todd stopped chewing the bite he'd just taken. Maddie thought she'd never seen his eyes grow so large.

Jack parked his Acura in the driveway. He saw Maddie's truck alone in the garage; of course, her husband was gone. *What was his name? Ron?*

The house was a broad, ranch style home on a large lot. The heavy wood-shingled roof needed some repair, but overall the home was appealing and comfortable looking. Jack could see Maddie rushing about through the kitchen window. He smiled involuntarily.

Todd answered the door.

"You all ready, sport?"

"Yup. Mom said I could bring my camera to get some shots of the game."

"You bet. Good idea. Bring a jacket too, they keep that place pretty cold."

"Right." Todd bounded up the stairs toward his room.

Maddie joined Jack in the entryway. "Hi there. Seems like I'm always thanking you for something."

"Well, maybe one of these days you'll get a chance to pay me back." *I wish*, Jack thought, watching Maddie as she adjusted the collar on Todd's jacket.

She caught him looking and he turned to the door.

"We'd better get going. The freeways are not much fun this time of night. We'll call if it gets late," he said over his shoulder.

"Bye Mom!" Todd called, scrambling into the front seat of Jack's car. "Wow, leather!" he exclaimed just before slamming the car door.

"You all strapped in there?" Jack asked, looking across at Todd.

"Yup. Been strapped in all my life," he said, "according to Mom."

"Yeah, well, she's a good mom."

"The best." The conviction in Todd's voice impressed Jack. He looked over at the boy again, noting that he looked nothing like Maddie with his dark brown hair and eyes. *Must look like Rod.*

The only thing better than the rink-side seats was getting to meet two of the players after the game. And in watching Todd's excitement, Jack felt the thrill also.

"So Jack, this is your son?" The team captain wanted to know as they posed for a photo with Todd.

"No, afraid not. But he's a good friend of mine, and a true Kings fan."

"All right," the assistant captain grinned, clapping Todd on the back. "You come back soon, eh?"

Todd beamed, nodding.

He said nothing on the way to the car.

"You okay, pal?" Jack asked as they got on the freeway.

"I think I'm in shock," Todd replied with a smile. "I didn't know you *knew* the Kings." In his lap he held the precious camera in one hand, an autographed puck in the other. "Mom'll be so excited."

"Speaking of Mom, we'd better give her a call. Can you dial for me?" Jack handed Todd his cell phone, and Todd punched in the numbers.

"MOM! You'll never guess…"

They arrived home without incident, and Maddie sent Todd upstairs to get ready for bed.

"He got kind of quiet on the way home. I hope he wasn't upset about anything," Jack told Maddie at the door.

"I'm sure he's exhausted. One thing I *do* know about hockey, that guy he met is his favorite player."

"Oh." Jack pretended to scratch the corner of his eye. "Good." He paused, choosing his next words carefully. "I thought maybe he was thinking about his dad."

"I, uh…doubt that." Maddie pushed a loose strand of hair behind her ear.

"Well, I'd never want to interfere. You let me know if I overstep, okay?"

"Sure. Don't worry about that. You couldn't possibly."

Jack thought her comment a little strange, but had to let it go. There would be no more conversation tonight.

In the car on the way back to his townhouse, Jack pondered Todd's relationship with his father. Something had bothered him from the start, and he couldn't put his finger on it. Something Todd had said at lunch that day in the commissary. They were talking about Todd's interests, and…

Ray. He had called his father "Ray" instead of "Dad." And Maddie had not corrected him. Jack shook his head ruefully.

My pop would have whooped me good had I called him by his given name.

The Acura's clock read 1 a.m. as Jack parked in his

garage. Glancing around for his jacket, he noticed the cell phone Todd had left on the passenger seat. It was still displaying Todd's home phone number. With a grin, Jack pressed "Save".

Four

Maddie lay back in the tub and let the hot water rise up to her chin. She didn't care that her hair, most of which was piled on top of her head with a clip, was getting wet. The water soothed her, and she'd put on some soft music to calm her nerves. She thought about lighting some candles, deciding finally that it was a silly indulgence. The bath salts smelled of magnolias, and she closed her eyes to let her mind wander.

It was Sunday night, and three weeks had passed since she'd said good night to Jack at her front door. In that three weeks, Ray had returned home, Todd had made the "A" team in soccer, and the cookies she'd baked for open house had been a sweet, profitable, success. Paul had hired two new assistants, so her workload had eased a little. Now she could get back to researching civil law instead of answering the phones.

Her truck was in the shop being aligned and getting a nav system installed, more for Todd's enjoyment than her own need; she never went anywhere new. She thought about Della, one of the new girls, and how she'd invited Maddie out with a couple of her friends after work. Della gave her a lift home Friday night and made the offer on the way. Now she wished she'd gone. Ray had been distant and aloof since his return from Colorado.

She lifted her big toe from the water to meet a droplet of water hanging from the tap. Her thoughts turned to Todd. Todd, too, had been different lately, more reserved and less animated when he was around the house. In the yard, or playing in the street with his friend Bryan, Todd behaved as boisterous as ever. It worried her, but she couldn't quite figure out what was wrong.

The thought she avoided, of course, was that of Jack. She couldn't expect to hear from him, she reasoned, why should he call? She splashed her foot back into the water with disdain. She should not be wasting her time thinking about Jack McKenzie.

But the thing that bothered her the most, the thorn in her side that would not go away, was the fact that Ray did not touch her when he came home, nor since.

She remembered times, times when Ray couldn't wait to get her alone. Especially after having been away so long. Those nights of intimate and loving foreplay, wine glasses on the nightstand and lacy red and black teddies. She blushed at the memory. When was the last time she surprised Ray with a new negligee? A dab of cologne on her neck? When did he stop bringing her souvenirs and airport trinkets?

Maddie closed her eyes and drifted in and out of twilight. The slam of the front door startled her and she turned to read the clock on the bathroom counter. It was 8 p.m. and Ray was just getting in from God knows where. *He was at the gym, he'll say*, but a tiny voice inside her said it would be a lie.

She didn't bother dressing. Throwing on a white terry robe, she met him in the kitchen, her damp hair in waves. He was pawing through Saturday's mail, and looked up without a word when she entered.

"Long day," she commented, crossing her arms and leaning against the counter.

"Who the hell is this?"

Maddie started at the irritation in his voice. In his hand were photos that Todd had printed off earlier in the day. She drew closer for a better look. There was Todd and Jack flanked by two Los Angeles Kings hockey players.

She snatched the photos from Ray's hands and placed them back on the counter.

"It's Jack and Todd, of course," she sniffed. "These are Todd's."

"Jack who?"

Maddie was standing close enough to catch a whiff of alcohol on Ray's breath. Further incensed, she bridled. "He's a friend. I told you about him," she snapped. "We went to school together." She kept her comments short, afraid she might say something she'd later regret. But it was too late.

"Well, isn't that sweet." Ray opened the refrigerator and grabbed a bottle of white wine. He didn't offer her any; he poured himself a tumbler-full and turned to face her.

"You might as well know right now. I'm going to Switzerland."

Maddie could feel her face pale. Again. *Again. He's leaving.*

"It's a major assignment. We're taking photographers up. It'll be about a month. I'm only going to ask you once if you'll come with me. We can take the kid out of school."

Maddie's tongue seemed to swell with her anger. She didn't know what made her more furious, the part about asking her only once, or his referral to Todd as "the kid."

"Well, I'm only going to tell you once, Ray, have a great time." Her voice was low and surprisingly calm.

"Fine. But let me tell you something. Someday you're

going to realize that it means nothing, nothing at all to that boy up there, what you do for him. He's spoiled, he's a mama's boy and he can't do a damned thing for himself. You're going to wake up having lived your whole damned life for him and for what? He'll up and leave you, and marry some other little mama to take care of him. And you, my dear, will be all alone." Ray took a long draught of wine.

"And why is that, Ray? I thought we were going to grow old together. Will you still be on the mountain, then?" Maddie approached him, her tone edged with fury.

"Most likely. I can't fit in here, Madelyn. To tell you the truth, this life here bores the hell out of me. I've tried…"

"Oh, right. You've tried. Sure." Maddie fought hard not to cry. His words were so hurtful, so full of lies and anger. And why? What had she ever done but try to be a good wife and mother?

"You've been a terrible father. You never even try to get closer to Todd. All you care about is your damned mountains."

"Yeah, that's what it's all about, isn't it Maddie? Todd. Always Todd. You don't want a husband; you want a father for Todd. And I failed. Well, I'm sorry I can't be the kind of father you have in mind. I don't have a PhD in Parenthood! Maybe you should just quit worrying about it, because it seems to me you're a pretty good mother and father both. I sure as hell am not going to worry about it anymore."

With that he downed the rest of the wine and left the room. Maddie followed him up the stairs to their bedroom, where Ray was pulling a suitcase off the shelf. She watched numbly as he threw a few items into it, passing through the bathroom to collect his razor and toiletries.

"Ray, what's this all about?"

"It's no good, Maddie. I don't want to be here anymore.

Here, I am guilty all the time. Out there, I am on top of the world. Don't you get it?"

He paused to stare at her, searching her face for a response. Her eyes filled with the tears she'd kept in check until now. Until the realization of Ray's intention had slapped her hard across the heart.

At the front door, he turned to look back through the house. Then he turned to Maddie once more.

"Tell the kid I said good-bye. This isn't his fault; I hope you will tell him that at least. I'll…I'll be back for the rest of my things. Good luck, Madelyn." He stared at her evenly for another moment, his blue eyes dark, moist and bloodshot.

Maddie started to protest but was too choked up. She watched Ray drag the suitcase to the driveway and throw it into the back seat of his Jeep. And then he was gone.

She began to cry. Softly at first, then loudly, crashing her fists down on the kitchen counter, then the table, then the wall. A kind of hysteria overtook her, the weeks of strain having finally built into a tremendous wave of self-pity and regret. Drowning her.

"Hello?" Jack's voice was thick with sleep. He'd been asleep for two hours, having been up the entire night before building a model.

"Jack?"

Jack squinted at his watch. It was only 9 p.m. Shaking his head to clear it, he sat up on the couch.

"Hello?"

"Jack? It's Todd." *Todd. Todd?*

"Todd! What's up, son?"

"I was just wondering if—do you think maybe you could come over here for a little while?" The boy's voice was tinged with thinly disguised grief, and Jack became immediately focused.

"Come over? Gee, what's going on? You having a party?"

"Not exactly. My mom's kinda freaking out. I thought maybe you could come over and help."

Now alarmed at Todd's words, Jack stood up. "Freaking out how, Todd?"

"She's-she's—" Todd paused, and the sounds coming from the receiver were momentarily muffled until he spoke again. "She's sad. I need you to come over, Jack. Please. You can cheer her up. She won't stop crying."

Jack frowned. "Todd, is your dad there?"

"Ray? He's gone. He made Mom cry. Are you coming, Jack?"

"I'm on my way, pal. You just sit tight, and don't worry. Everything will be okay."

Pausing only to splash some cold water on his face and pop a breath mint, Jack was out the door.

Maddie did stop crying, and poured herself a glass of wine. She sat down, miserable, at the kitchen table and tried to straighten out her thoughts. She knew the wine wouldn't help there, but thought it might ease a little of the pain.

Todd came in, and she reached out her arm for him. There was no longer any reason to shelter him from the truth.

"Ray's gone," she said simply.

"I know." He hugged his mother, his face hesitant and worried. "Mom, I sorta did something. Don't be mad, okay?"

"Mad?" As if anything could change the way she felt right now. She stroked Todd's hair away from his forehead. "Now what could be so bad that I could get mad at you?"

He looked into his mother's face, and Maddie knew he

could see all the pain and grief reflected there, her reddened, swollen eyes and wet cheeks. He dropped a wrinkled business card on the table and wiped his own eye with the corner of his sleeve. Then, taking a deep breath, he drew himself up to his tallest and closed his eyes briefly. "I called Jack," he said finally. "And," Todd went on, swallowing hard, "he's coming over. Um, now."

Maddie's eyes opened wide. "No, you didn't."

"Yes, I did. He can make us feel better, Mom. He'll make us laugh. You'll see."

Maddie sighed. "Okay, honey. Okay." Wearily, she got up and together they went upstairs.

Quickly she pulled a soft, velour caftan over her head and then washed her face. And that was all she had time for before she saw the Acura's headlights turn into the driveway. Todd had retreated to his room.

She opened the door and neither of them spoke, at first. Both felt awkward, and finally Maddie stepped back, pulling the door open wide.

"I'm sorry. Please come in. Todd told me he called you, and I'm so sorry he bothered you."

"No, it's fine, really. Are…are you okay?" he asked, trying to look into her face as she breezed past him into the kitchen.

"Sure. No." She picked up her wine. "Would you like…?"

"No thanks."

Finally she stopped moving long enough to notice his gaze. *He's looking for bruises.* Forcing a brief grin, Maddie squared her shoulders. "If you're looking for abuse, you won't find it on the outside. It's not like that."

"What happened?"

"He's gone. He left. He's off to Switzerland."

"Switzerland? You mean, on a climb?"

"I mean, for good. He's gone for good, Jack."

"Did he say he was leaving you?"

"He didn't have to." Maddie felt her eyes beginning to fill again. "Oh God."

"Maddie, people say things when they're mad that they don't mean, you know? Maybe things will get better," he offered lamely. "You'll talk it out."

"No, he meant these things. And I meant the things I said. It's over, Jack. We blew it. We couldn't, *I* couldn't hold it together. What am I going to do?" She began to pace, to cry openly, wringing her hands in hopelessness. The wave was crashing down again.

Obviously unable to stand her pain any longer, Jack reached for her and pulled her into his arms. This gesture unleashed a fresh torrent of tears, and she cried into his shirt as she pressed her fists against his chest.

"How am I going to do this?" she sobbed. "It's not fair."

"Do what?"

"How can I raise Todd all alone?"

A puzzled look on his face, Jack stroked her hair. "Don't worry about that right now. Everything will work out. Really."

She cried for a time, and then pulled away from him, embarrassed and uncomfortable. Something about the way Jack held her, his long, sensitive fingers cupping her head against his chest that scared her. It felt too good. Too good to believe. And in her vulnerable, hurting condition, it would be just too easy to make a mistake. Another mistake she could not afford.

"Look, Jack, I'm really sorry about all this."

"Don't be. I consider you my friend. I'm glad Todd

called me. I'm glad he trusted me that much. Is he upset about Ray?"

"Of course. Why don't you go upstairs and say hello to him. He'd be glad to see you."

Jack took her advice and went upstairs in search of Todd's room. He found Todd on the bed watching TV.

"Jack!" Todd started toward him, and then paused, holding back. Too big for a hug, Jack decided.

"Hey, bud, what's up?" Jack punched him playfully on the shoulder.

"Is Mom okay?"

"Sure. She's fine."

Jack looked around the room, smiling at the posters and artwork and science awards. On the dresser were more trophies and two framed pictures. The first was of Maddie and Ray, apparently on their wedding day. Looking radiant and happy, Maddie stood beside Ray, waving from the bow of the Renaissance, a nineteenth century schooner rented out at the marina for special events. Jack had staged a music video on the boat a few years back. Looking closely, Jack stared hard at the face of a man who could walk out on a woman like Maddie. He felt his teeth grind.

The other photo was of a man with a round face and jovial smile beneath a full mustache. His hair was thick and wavy, and like his eyes, was dark brown. The grainy photo, possibly enlarged from a snapshot, was signed, "Love, Papa." It was most likely Todd's grandfather; they had the same eyes.

Jack turned back to Todd. "Whatcha watching?"

"An old movie. *Field of Dreams*."

"I always liked that one. Kevin Costner, right?"

"Yeah. The dad is really cool, except his name is Ray."

Jack chuckled. "Do you know how many movie bad guys are named Jack?"

Todd smiled. "Heroes, too."

"Maybe. You, uh, you gonna be okay?"

"Yeah."

"Okay. I gotta take off. I'm working on this huge project, and if I'm ever gonna have time to go to another hockey game, I've got to get cracking. And thanks," he said, bumping his fist against Todd's shoulder, "for calling me."

"Sure, Jack."

Back downstairs, Maddie waited by the door.

"Well, here I go again," she began, preparing to once more offer thanks.

"Uh-Uh. Shhh." Jack pressed a single finger to her lips. "You get a good night's sleep. Things will look different in the morning."

"Okay," she mouthed, attempting to smile.

Popping a quick kiss on her forehead, Jack hurried out the door and into his car.

Jack lay in his bed, unable to sleep despite the hour and his exhaustion. He needed to start working again at 7 a.m., but he couldn't close his eyes. His thoughts stayed with Maddie and the interesting turn of events that had occurred.

The fact that Ray had left her changed everything. The three weeks that had passed since he'd seen her were tough. Weeks when he wondered about her, cared about—hell, *obsessed* over—her, and tried everything he could to forget about her. He'd just about succeeded in convincing himself that he should never see her again when Todd's call came, instantly bringing the fire back to life. Could she care about him? This thought gave Jack pause. She must have loved Ray, at least at one time. She'd married him, bore his child, stayed with him for how long? She'd mentioned at one time that she'd married right out of high school.

Wait a minute.

The photo on Todd's dresser, with Maddie dressed in white lace and veil…could not be.

Jack sprang from his bed and went to his file cabinet, flipping on the light as he walked. Rummaging through the many files of reference material, he pulled one, labeled "Renaissance," from the drawer. Inside was the promotional material on the three-masted ship now harbored in the marina.

Thumbing through the color brochure, he hunted for the information he needed. He'd made the video four years ago, and he could have sworn the ship had only been in service for four or five years at that time. Finally, he found the confirmation he was seeking. The Renaissance had been cruising the marina for only nine years.

Five

Miserably, Maddie dragged herself from bed on Monday morning. The shower helped but could not wash away the suffering of the night before, and she dressed with lethargy. Todd, too, was quiet, but his mood was more a reflection of hers than of his own.

Together they rushed out the front door, Maddie lugging her briefcase and Todd hastily stuffing his paper bag lunch into his backpack. Maddie stopped cold at the sight of the empty garage.

"The truck's in the shop," she murmured. Turning around, she quickly peered up the street toward the Reeds' house. Bryan's mother was just opening their garage door.

"Quick. Run up there and catch a ride," she commanded, and Todd took off at a brisk pace. Maddie watched until Bryan's mother waved that she would be glad to drive Todd to school.

Maddie walked slowly back into the house. She couldn't call in sick. Instead, she dialed Della's number. Hopefully, she would still be home.

There didn't seem to be any reason not to tell Della what happened. She would hear about it soon enough anyway.

"What a jerk." Della shook her head. "Some guys

should be boiled in hog fat."

Maddie nodded.

"Now maybe you'll go with us on Friday night." Della glanced over at Maddie. "He's not worth it, you know. The way I figure it, most of us are better off without men. Bunch of louts. Except maybe for Johnny Depp"

Maddie broke a brief smile. Della was right, of course. Johnny would never say the things Ray had said.

At work, Maddie dug into her research with fervor. It was the only place she could be without doubts about her uncertain future. She started working past quitting time, and only went home for Todd's sake. He already spent too much time with Bryan's family, who kept him after school every day.

For two weeks she went about this new routine until one night Paul found her in the firm's library, hunched over several law journals.

"Maddie, it's time to go. I'm locking up."

"I have a key, Paul. I just need to finish this last report."

"You've been working too much, kiddo. It's time to lighten up a little. Get out, enjoy yourself some."

Maddie looked upon Paul with kindness. She had been more than lucky to land a position with his firm. "Okay. I'm going."

"Good. And take tomorrow morning off. I don't want to see you here before eleven."

Maddie nodded. Perhaps she did need a break.

There was a time when Maddie rejoiced over every new bloom. From the deep red American Beauty to the bright yellow Graceland, her roses were a source of both tranquility and pride. Now, on her hands and knees in the rose garden behind her house, she sighed as she found aphids picnicking on the green foliage. Focused intensely on pruning the long neglected plants, she at last stood up, satisfied, and brushed off her jeans. Looking around the yard, she saw several signs of deterioration and it saddened her. Like her marriage, her once beautiful home was beginning to decay.

She needed to check the clock. It may already be time to go to work; she had misplaced her watch. Pulling off her cotton gloves she went inside through the back kitchen door and almost missed the blinking light on the answering machine. With some hesitation, she pressed *play*, hoping it was not her husband.

"Maddie, it's Jack. I called your office and they said you were at home, but you're…not. What I called about is, well—oh, hell. I want to take you to dinner Friday night. I'll pick you up at seven. These reservations are hard to get, so you can't say no. Bye."

Friday! Day after tomorrow. Dinner with Jack. She played the message again, hypnotized by the sound of his voice. Warm, comically demanding, undertones of modesty. So typically Jack. Was there any reason she should not go? *He considers himself my friend. And right now, that counts a lot.*

"I've got to get a new dress," she murmured happily.

Maddie turned around before her dresser mirror. This was a good idea. The proverbial "little black dress" that could go anywhere. It flattered her without drawing too much attention.

"You look great, Mom." Todd watched as she assessed her appearance.

"You think so?"

"Yup. Jack will like it."

She rushed over to her son and gave him a quick hug, then went back to the dresser in search of earrings. "Are Bryan and Mike on their way?"

"I don't know why dopey Mike has to come. Me and Bryan can stay by ourselves."

Maddie turned and gave her son a wistful smile. "I know. But Bryan's mom insisted they both come. Try to put up with him. Sixteen-year-olds think they're pretty cool."

The ringing of the phone forced a closure to the subject. "Hello?" she answered brightly, expecting Jack's voice to respond.

"Hello Maddie. I need to talk to you."

The smile slid from her face. Todd's gladness faded with his mother's and he grew wary.

"Ray. Can we make it another time?"

"No. I'm coming over. We need to talk about some things."

"Now is definitely not a good time. Tomorrow would be much better." She hung up the phone. She would not let Ray spoil her evening.

As always, Jack was right on time. He asked Maddie to turn for him in the kitchen, nodding his head.

"Very nice," he said. "The dress is okay, too."

Maddie made a mock frown.

"I'll just get my coat and say good-bye to the boys," she called over her shoulder and dashed up the stairs.

"Now just stay inside. Mike, there's a pizza in the freezer if you guys want it…keep the doors locked. I'll be home…well, I'm not sure, but it won't be too late. I have my phone in my purse. And of course you can always call

Mrs.—"

"Yes, *Mother*," Todd replied, mocking the "good" boy he was supposed to be. "We'll be fine and won't burn the house down. We have to finish our projects for the fair tomorrow."

"What fair?"

"The *science* fair. I told you about it! We have to be at school at 8:30 to set it up. But don't worry, Bryan's mom is going to pick us up, just in case you're still asleep."

Maddie smiled at her son. He'd grown up so suddenly.

Back in the kitchen she picked up her purse just as the front door swung open so hard that its knob hit the wall. Ray Tyler strode in and surveyed the room, his intense blue eyes fixing Jack in their stunned gaze.

"Sorry to interrupt."

Momentarily stunned, Maddie glanced quickly at Jack's surprised and wary expression. She eventual found her voice.

"Ray, I told you not to come. I'm going out."

"So I see. Well, no reason to waste any time, is there?" He approached Jack and extended his hand. "Ray Tyler."

Hesitantly Jack shook Ray's hand. "Jack McKenzie."

"If you don't mind, Jack, I need to speak to my wife for a few minutes."

Without a word, Maddie left the room and Ray followed her to the den, where he shut the door behind him.

"I just needed to tell you a few things," he began.

"Make it fast, okay?"

Ray ran his fingers along the edge of the bookcase against the wall, looking remotely like he'd never seen it before. He took a moment to compose his words, not looking Maddie in the eye.

"I'm sorry you feel I've let Todd down. I never meant

to ignore him, Maddie. We're just different. I could never begin to be—" The angry pout on Maddie's lips gave him pause. "You know what I mean. You wouldn't have let me even try, and you know it. He's a great kid. I've always cared a lot about him. I just don't want you to think otherwise."

Maddie's resolve weakened. Why couldn't he have said these things before? When they still mattered?

"Anyway, I'll be taking my things soon. I leave for Switzerland next Friday."

"Is that all?" Maddie asked softly.

"Yeah. Except that, I'm really sorry about everything. I was drunk before, I was tough on you, I know. It isn't your fault. We just stopped connecting awhile back." He rubbed his forehead, looking briefly away from her.

Maddie held back tears that threatened to ruin her perfectly applied make up. Confusion fogged her mind. The sincerity in Ray's voice reminded her of another time, another Ray Tyler. The Ray she'd loved, the Ray she'd somehow lost.

"Thanks," was all she could manage.

She walked him back to the entryway; upon seeing Jack waiting in the kitchen, Ray seemed to grow colder.

"You kids have a nice time," he said with a false grin before walking out the door.

The restaurant was on the top of Wilder's Pass, just south of the valley. The city lay out before them as they dined, looking very much, Maddie thought, like a blanket of twinkling Christmas lights. They made a silent agreement not to talk about Ray or the unpleasantness that had preceded their evening.

"So. Do your folks still live around here?" Maddie asked.

"Nope. They moved to Palm Springs a couple of years ago, thank God! I see them once in a while…not enough I suppose. They call. I'm the bad son, I guess."

Maddie smiled. "That's right, you have a couple of brothers, don't you?"

"One brother, Sean, and my cousin-turned-brother, Case. Casey's the big important doctor, and Sean's the big important college dean."

"And you're the big important artist."

"I might as well be a spud farmer." Jack paused, then chuckled at his own joke. "While we were growing up, all we heard about was potatoes. And, 'go to school, get a degree, get a good job'."

"You have a good job," Maddie began, lightly touching the back of Jack's hand.

"You have to understand, nothing about me pleases my dad. The latest is, he's ashamed that I didn't marry Kelly." He shook his head. "Damned good thing I didn't."

"I'm sure he loves you. My father was Irish, too. He had a lot of trouble showing his feelings."

"Oh, my pop never has trouble showing his feelings. Uh uh. He's very…demonstrative. I still have the scars," Jack offered with a sardonic chuckle.

"He beat you?"

"It was a necessary part of our upbringing, you see. Dad was military. WWII. Of course, today, he'd be behind bars."

Maddie bit her lip at the thought. "That's terrible. Your brother, too?"

"Sure. It wasn't that bad. He's not a bad guy, it's just the way he was raised."

"Gosh, I couldn't imagine striking Todd. To me, it's just teaching kids violence."

"Kids. Yeah. But this went on until I was seventeen. Until I was bigger and stronger than he was." Jack shook his head, his eyes seeing another time and place. "One thing's for sure, I'll never hit my son."

Now, placing his hand over hers, his expression cleared. "What about you, your father's gone?"

"Yes, my father died, gosh, ten years ago, and Mom died last year."

"I'm so sorry."

"Yeah, me too," she said sadly. "It's been tough. Seems like the last several years have been so…nothing. Just blank. I can't describe it."

"You don't have to." His eyes told Maddie he knew where she'd been, that he'd been there, too. "But it gets better from here."

"Think so?"

"Know so."

His confidence was contagious, and Maddie felt a glow of anticipation for the future. And besides, he was holding her hand. She felt bold. "So, where did you meet Kelly?"

"At the studios. Did I mention that she's an actress?"

"You may have, but I knew."

"How?"

"She gave an interview to some TV industry rag I picked up at the dentist's office. She mentioned your name."

Jack groaned. "When she snagged that role on *Morning Star*, she kind of flipped out. Big celebrity now. Personally, I think soap operas are pretty much drivel. Did she mention Duncan, too?"

"Not by name. Only that she would start the show in a few months and the baby would be older by then. Something about moving to New York."

Jack's grip tightened on her hand. "Yeah, well, we'll

see about that." He stood, prompting Maddie to stand also. "C'mon. Let's take a walk." They strolled out onto the large deck and gardens surrounding the restaurant.

"This was wonderful, Jack. It feels so good to do normal things again. I really needed to get out."

"I know," he said quietly, his eyes perusing the sky. "It looks like rain."

Cold descended on them. Jack slipped his jacket off and placed it around her shoulders, then walked her toward the parking lot and his car. It was a simple gesture, one that Maddie had not experienced in many years. She didn't realize it was still okay for a man to be a gentleman.

Soon they were on the freeway, and the heater brought warmth back to Maddie's legs. Briefly she closed her eyes, savoring the feeling, the smooth vibration of the car's tires and the soft melodics of John Coltrane on the satellite radio. She could almost forget the ugly scene that had played out with Ray, almost forget that she would soon be a single mother. Indeed, she could almost forget that anything existed beyond the safety and comfort of Jack's car.

It was his voice that pulled her back to the present and the reality that they were heading down the off-ramp, an unhappy reminder that their evening was about to end. Except that Jack was suggesting something else.

"Would you be offended if I asked you over for…coffee or something?"

His offer both excited and scared her. She felt she knew him, at the same time knowing that she didn't. Not really. But did it matter?

Maddie stole a sideways glance at Jack. The headlights from the car behind them lit his eyes, reflected by the rear view mirror. He seemed so sincere, so honest, and so trust-worthy. Sensing her gaze, he looked at her briefly and smiled.

"Nothing to figure out, Maddie. I just thought you might like to talk some more."

"Sure. I'd love to."

"It's two bedrooms and a loft. When I moved here I thought I would use the loft for a studio, but it's kind of a junk heap right now. So the other bedroom ended up being the studio." He gave her a brief tour. In the second bedroom, a large table stood in the middle of the room supporting a model in process. Maddie was impressed.

"That's for DeCaprio's next film. He's a WWII pilot, that's the inside of a command post." Jack waved his hand toward the drafting table on one wall, which was stacked with books, many of them opened to WWII scenes. "There's a lot of research involved, obviously. Some nights I am perfectly bleary-eyed. And that," he said, pointing to a computer on a table against one wall, "is my best friend and my worst enemy."

"What's in there?" Maddie asked, pointing to a closed door adjacent to the room they were leaving.

"Just my bedroom." He opened the door just a crack and peeked in. "Okay, it's safe." He threw the door open and turned on the light. "Couldn't remember if I'd made my bed."

Maddie giggled. The smile on Jack's face was one of those she adored, simple, honest and candid.

This room was tastefully decorated in earth tones and subtle African patterns. A bed, a highboy, a small writing desk. A master bathroom and a closet.

"No TV?" she asked in surprise.

"Not in here. Watching TV in bed is against my religion." He gave her a subtle wink and switched the light off.

His living room was contemporary but he claimed not to like it. "I'm more a casual guy. Let's just say I was unfairly influenced. I think I was trying to look like something I'm not. Now I hate it, especially because of why I did it." He left her for the kitchen, calling over his shoulder. "Coffee or wine? Sparkling water, 7-UP, raisin juice?"

Maddie giggled and unzipped her boots, standing them near the door. She, too, regarded the white carpeting, white sofa and tan leather chair with disdain, choosing instead to sit on the floor beside the glass coffee table. She'd never met Kelly, but now, this decor embodied her.

"Surprise me," she called back, smiling to herself. Somehow she knew he'd pick something she would like. He wasn't gone long before she heard him behind her, working to build a small fire in the fireplace. Then he returned to the kitchen.

Through the sliding glass doors she could see the rain beginning to fall. So his prediction had been correct. From Jack's hillside townhouse, there was an abbreviated view of the city below, and as the rain ran down the windows the lights became a colorful, blurry, mosaic.

"Here you go," he offered, squatting down to hand her a tall, steaming mug. She took a tentative sip.

"MMMmm. Bailey's and coffee! I love it."

"Aye, and what kind of an Irishman would I be without a bit of Irish Cream on hand?"

Indeed, it was perfect for a chilly night. She scooted herself across the carpeting to sit by the fire, and Jack joined her with his own cup.

There was nothing to say, at first, so she continued to sip the coffee and stare at the fire.

"What's on your mind?" he asked, waving his hand slightly to get her attention.

"Nothing, really. Just enjoying the moment."

"Ah. Good. I was hoping you weren't worrying about what happened at the house earlier."

"No. I refuse to worry about it. It's Ray's problem."

Jack nodded slowly. "Well, I just hope I didn't make things any worse for you."

"No, you didn't. Quite the contrary. I'm glad you were there."

Jack nodded again and put his mug down on the hearth.

"Hey. I have something I want to try." He took her mug from her hands and put it beside his. "Wanna do a little experiment?" His mischievous grin charmed her.

"What kind of experiment?"

"More like an exercise. An exercise in trust. Do you trust me?"

"Of course I do."

"Are you sure?" His eyes were merry.

"Well, sure I'm sure. I'm here, aren't I? Didn't I trust you to take my only son away for an evening of violence and bloodshed?" Maddie smiled back.

"Okay, okay. Let's just see. I want you to close your eyes, and…," he began, reaching for her hand, "relax."

Almost timidly she extended her arm and placed her hand in his. His was warmer, both soft and strong, and he grasped hers firmly. She closed her eyes.

"Good. Now, this is about trust and honesty. Can you trust me with your honesty?"

She didn't answer, but felt like she might start giggling at any moment.

"How does that feel?" he asked, now using both his hands to gently massage hers. Back and forth, his fingers traced the lines, the patterns, the soft depths of her palm.

"It feels good."

"Good? Okay. I guess that'll do. Anything else?"

Maddie just grinned.

"Maybe I need to make this a little more challenging." Lacing his fingers with hers, he drew her hand to his face, gently sliding the back of it along his cheek. Her smile softened and her face began to color. With his free hand, he caressed her face in the same manner.

"Now how does it feel? Or rather, how do *you* feel?"

"I feel…good."

"Tell me more."

"I feel…warm."

"Better."

Carefully he opened her hand and now placed her palm against his cheek. She could feel heat, and the beginning of tomorrow's beard. And then her fingers seemed to come alive, moving without his help to his lips, softly tracing their shape. Jack was very still, and Maddie wondered if he was watching her face as she touched him.

"And now—now what are you thinking?" His question intruded; Maddie uttered a short gasp, swallowed, and then moistened her lips. There was a word forming in her mind, a word with which she was not comfortable. Perhaps she was wrong.

"I feel…like I'm not really here."

"Is it uncomfortable? Is it scary? Is it…a good feeling?"

"Scary," she whispered.

"Don't be afraid," Jack said, briefly brushing back her hair with his fingertips.

At his touch Maddie opened her eyes and pulled away in confusion. The wine they'd shared at dinner, the coffee, the rain, the fire, all served to drag her into a swirling, dizzying pool, rendering her light-headed and off balance.

"I'm sorry," he said, smiling, his own confusion evident.

"Don't be." She picked up her coffee and Jack could see she was trembling. "Your point is well taken."

"My point? I'm not sure I had one," he replied, sipping from his own mug. "I don't know—*didn't know*—what I expected."

"Well, sometimes you think you can trust someone, but in the end, you can't." She stood up and went to retrieve her boots. "I think I'd like to go home now, okay?"

"Sure." Jack hastily got to his feet and began putting out the fire.

The drive back to Maddie's house was quiet, neither quite sure what to say. In her driveway, Jack shut off the car and sat staring ahead at the dark house. Maddie gathered her purse and made a tentative reach for the door handle.

"I'll see you inside," Jack said.

"It's okay, Jack."

"No, I insist. I want to make sure everything's okay."

Mike Reed was stretched out on the couch. "The dudes are asleep upstairs, we ate the 'za, nobody called." He stood, pulled on his jacket and sauntered to the front door. Jack slipped the teen some cash and Mike took his leave.

Maddie waited beside the door. "Thanks for a wonderful evening. I had a great time."

He eyed her thoughtfully, restraining his true inclinations and substituting those of a friend. The friend he had proclaimed to be. "Let me know how things go, okay? And say hi to Todd."

"Sure."

"Look, Maddie, I…I didn't mean to offend you tonight. I know I was treading on thin ice. But please know something…you really can trust me. I would never hurt you." He grimaced inwardly at the triteness of his words. "Good night. Call if you need me."

She nodded, holding her hands tightly behind her back. Jack brushed her forehead ever so briefly with his lips before dashing out into the rain.

Maddie closed the door and sank back against it with a deep, anguished sigh. If he only knew, she thought. It had nothing to do with his trustworthiness, everything to do with her ability to trust anyone at all. Especially herself. She felt foolish, wishing she had been able to tell him how she really felt. But it had been so, so very long since any feelings like these filled her head…her heart…so very full.

Slowly she raised her hand to her face, gently touching her forehead and then her own lips with the same fingers that had traced his before.

She felt utterly, profoundly alone. And the thought came to her, the word she could not say to Jack, the same word that had come to her while those fingers caressed his lips. The word was *seduction.*

Six

"Mom! Mom! Wake up!" Todd stood beside the bed, excitedly waving both hands near her face. The sun streamed in through the window over the bed, and Maddie groaned. Not usually annoyed by her son, she bit her lip to keep from saying something she'd regret.

"I'm home! Look, I won a medal!"

Maddie sat up. The clock hands hovered close to the eleven and she couldn't tell, through her haze, whether it was almost noon or an hour earlier.

"Wow. Um, that's great, honey."

Todd noticed the tissue box and two or three balled up tissues on the bed. "Are you okay, Mom? Are you sick?"

Maddie followed his gaze and quickly swept the tissues up. "No, I just got a runny nose last night. You know how, when it's really cold out, your nose can run?"

"Did you have a good time with Jack?" Todd was now unconcerned with the Kleenex and was holding his medal up to the light.

"Yes. We went for a bite to eat." She never lied to Todd, but in this case a little bend to the truth was appropriate. She disappeared into the bathroom before he could ask her more. "He said to tell you hi. Have you had breakfast?" she called through the door.

"Of course! Mom, it's almost noon! You must have been up late."

At this Maddie turned on the shower, drowning out any further admonitions.

Despite the alcohol (or maybe because of it, she later thought,) she'd lain awake half the night. She thought Jack might call and give her a chance to apologize. She even thought Ray might call. Twice she'd picked up the phone to be sure it still worked.

After hearing Todd's triumphant tale of winning the science fair medal, Maddie watched the day slide quietly by. Still the phone did not ring.

Jack woke with a head full of cement. Setting the water as hot as he could tolerate, he showered and washed his hair. *Man!* he thought. Too much wine, too much coffee, too much… Like his computer so often did, Jack's brain locked up at the thought he wanted to avoid.

In the kitchen he brewed a cup of espresso and sat down with the Saturday paper. The coffee would diminish his headache; he had a strong distaste for pain medication, feeling he'd had more than his share during his years of playing hockey.

Turning the pages of the newspaper, he found it difficult to focus on anything in particular. His mind kept returning to Maddie, and each time he consciously swept the thoughts away.

"Damn." Maybe he just wasn't ready to dive back into the dating pool. What was it about Madelyn Cross anyway? Madelyn *Tyler*, he reminded himself, and his thoughts turned to Ray and his rude interruption the night before.

"I have enough problems," he murmured. *I don't need to get involved with someone who has even more.*

But the fact remained. Maddie intrigued him, and he was certain she felt the same. There was something there. She was a special person, someone he could really get close to. And despite the fact that his "better" judgment told him otherwise, he knew he would continue to pursue her.

Having decided thus, Jack folded the paper. In the studio, his mega-model wasn't getting done by itself.

By Sunday afternoon Maddie had all the quiet she could stand. Staring with disdain at the last load of laundry, she shook her head. It could wait. She sought Todd out and they left the house for a long walk.

Behind the house was a vast field of undeveloped land. The title, she'd heard, was tangled in litigation; the owner had died while in escrow with a real estate developer. Maddie was glad to hear it. The field afforded her property a lot of privacy. It was formerly a grazing pasture, and a small creek still ran near the perimeter on one side. Todd used to play in the creek as a young child.

Today, they walked along the creek and Todd reminisced about the frogs and pollywogs he'd caught there. Then he was quiet for a time, allowing each to return to their own thoughts. He picked up a pebble here and there, trying to skip it across the creek's surface.

"Hey Mom, did you know Jack has a little boy?"

"Yes. He's just a baby."

"He was saying how he'd like to bring him down here sometime to play."

"Well, that could be a while, you know. You'll be all grown up by the time Duncan is old enough to play down here."

Todd nodded and ran ahead, leaving Maddie to ponder the concept of having a grown son while Jack was trying to handle third grade with his.

Jack again. Thoughts of him still permeated her mind. Again and again she recalled the feel of his cheek, his lips, his breath on her hand. She blushed at the memory. What was he doing? Was the game to prove something, prove her attraction to him? Or was she meant to fail, meant to expose that she couldn't trust him or anyone else ever again?

Or perhaps, perhaps he *was* trying to seduce her.

On Monday, Todd went back to school and Maddie went back to work, her motivation lacking. It wasn't until the night before that she finally noticed Ray's things were missing. Most of his clothes, shoes and personal effects were gone. The kind of stuff that probably fit in the back seat of his Jeep. He'd be back, she imagined, for the large screen TV, and, of course, his skis and mountain equipment.

At her desk she struggled to finish her work. Every time Jack's face came to mind she shut it out and tried to think about Ray. Maybe she'd been too harsh. She could have tried harder to understand, to become more involved with his group. Maybe she just hadn't cared enough. Perhaps she should try to reach him, to talk some more, to forgive him.

At noon, Maddie turned down offers to go to lunch with the others. She'd brought a brown bag but didn't bother to retrieve it from the lunchroom, instead opting to again work through the hour alone in her office. When a shadow passed over her desk, she looked up to find Ray standing before her.

He was dressed in "nouveau business casual," his hands in his pockets as he looked around uneasily at the walls in the room.

"What are you doing here?" Maddie asked softly,

rising slowly to her feet.

"Thought you might want to have lunch." Ray cleared his throat. "I'm leaving Friday."

Maddie colored, looking down at her desk in disarray. She was afraid to look into his eyes. Remembering her regrets, her uncertainties, her fears, she decided she should talk to Ray and at least hear him out.

They walked a block to the Italian restaurant on the corner. Ray seemed nervous, yet determined to unload his thoughts, difficult as that might prove.

"I'm sorry I busted in on you the other night. When you told me not to come, I thought you were just mad."

"I should have told you I had a date."

Ray looked away, focusing his eyes on the street outside.

"I want you to know, you're the best woman I've ever known, Maddie. We had fun together. A lot of fun. You're beautiful, sexy, funny…"

"Ray, please. What are you trying to say?"

"Just that I don't regret a thing. Maybe we just weren't meant to be husband and wife. We're better off friends. Marriage just isn't—isn't for me. Not now." He paused for a sip of Chianti. "Look, I don't know what you think about this Jack guy. But when I get back from Europe, maybe you and I can get together sometime. Todd's getting older, he'll be able to go or not go…we could have some time alone."

Maddie stiffened slightly at Ray's reference to Todd, but she let it go. It didn't matter. It didn't matter because she knew she would not see Ray again. Not socially, anyway, and this was Ray's ultimate message. Having apologized, having talked about some kind of future relationship, Ray could go off to his mountain with a clear conscience. His arctic blue eyes said it all.

She stopped him at the entrance to her building.

"No need to come up. Have a nice trip." Her throat closing on her words, Maddie embraced Ray, weakly at first, then tightly, a good-bye embrace that embodied the sum total of her feelings. Almost desperately she tried to connect the near-stranger in her arms to the man she'd married, put her stock in, indeed, waged her future on. The door was really closing on that future, and their marriage. Ray hugged her back, whispering something into her ear that she could not understand, but she felt his implied apology.

Her spirits at an all-time low, she somehow drove herself home at five.

Todd was in the kitchen with a pan of frozen lasagna poised in his hands, the hot oven door open.

"Thought you might like pasta, Mom." He slid the pan inside, closed the oven, and then busied himself with plates and forks. He stopped briefly to accept his mother's grateful hug.

"You're a champ," she murmured, not having the heart to tell him what she'd had for lunch. "Any messages on the machine?"

"Uh…yeah. Some travel agent called. I left it on the machine so you could hear it."

"Nobody else?"

"Nope. Just a *hang-up*. No caller I.D."

Maddie listened to the message and jotted down the number. A glance at the clock told her that the agent was still in the office, so she dialed.

"Oh, Mrs. Tyler. Thanks for calling back. I was trying to reach your husband so I could give him a confirmation number. Since he changed his reservations so late, it would be a good idea for him to have that number in case of a mix-up."

"He changed them?"

"Yes, he called me yesterday to coordinate the replacement ticket for his associate, since you're unable to go."

"Oh, yes…" Maddie sat down and cleared her throat. "Could…could you read back the entire reservation to me? He'll want me to relay the information."

"Of course. Two tickets, Mr. Raymond Tyler and Mrs. Elise Hansen, non-stop on Swiss Air 5932, leaves LAX on Friday morning at 8 a.m. Tell him I was able to get seats together."

Maddie's mind raced dizzily. There was a question to ask, a question that posed a threat for which she was not prepared. She asked anyway.

"And the hotel reservation? Did you make that as well?"

"Certainly. The Hotel Schweizerhof. It's a suite, actually, in a lovely, older hotel with lots of charm."

"And for Mrs. Hansen?"

"Uh…let's see. I believe he said she would be making her own lodging accommodations."

"Thank you. I'll let him know." Carefully Maddie placed the phone back on its cradle.

Elise.

Elise Hansen was a new member of the climber's group to which Maddie and Ray had belonged for five years. Elise was the one who'd come over the night Todd developed pneumonia and had to be driven to the hospital. Ray was out of town, of course. Elise brought a casserole over when Maddie's mother had passed away last fall. Elise helped Maddie pick out the dress she'd worn to Ray's class reunion in January.

There was no reason for Elise Hansen to be accompanying Ray to Zurich. No *moral* reason. And yet, it did not appear as though Ray was making much effort to hide the fact.

Maddie didn't cry. Putting on a smile, she held her head up and went back to the kitchen to have dinner with the only male companion she could truly trust.

The week ended with a decided thud. Maddie stopped on her way home for their planned Friday night Chinese food, picking up Todd's usual favorites and her own. She was looking forward to chowing down and ordering a sad movie on demand. Maybe a bath, too.

The dark kitchen surprised her. On the counter was a note from Todd, saying he was at Bryan's and could he stay the night PLEEZE? Maddie smiled, and yet melancholy settled over her. A Friday night alone. By now, Ray and Elise would be landing in Switzerland.

She didn't bother to change clothes. Kicking off her shoes, she began to unload the Chinese food, wrinkling her nose at the sweet and sour chicken, Todd's preferred dinner. She would put it in the fridge for him to eat tomorrow. She poured herself a Coke and perused the phone list on the side of the cabinet for Bryan's phone number. Before she could dial, the phone rang. It would be her impatient son.

"Hello, sorry I'm late," she said, taking the phone across the kitchen to reach for a plate.

"Don't let it happen again."

The plate slipped to the floor and shattered. The voice was unmistakably Jack's, friendly, warm and chiding.

"Oh, hi…" Maddie answered, gingerly stepping around the chards of broken china. "I'm sorry, I thought you were Todd."

"Disappointed?" He didn't sound mad.

"Of course not." Maddie smiled in spite of herself, quickly walking to the laundry room in search of the broom.

"I'm not interrupting anything then?"

"No, no, I just got in. How are you?"

"Hungry. You wouldn't happen to have any sweet and sour chicken, would you?"

Maddie stopped in the laundry room doorway, her mind abuzz with surprise. *How…?* Then her eyes fell on Todd's note. Of course.

"Now what makes you think I'd have anything quite so special?" she teased.

"Just a guess." Maddie could almost see Jack's warm brown eyes.

"Hmmm. Well…it just so happens there's a little square box of sweet and sour chicken right in front of me. But you'd better be quick…"

"I can be there in ten minutes."

Ten minutes!

Maddie cleaned up the broken china then raced upstairs to change clothes. Suddenly, nothing seemed to feel right or look right, but nine minutes later she settled on her older jeans, the comfortable ones, and a lavender pullover sweater. She paused before her dresser mirror. What was she doing? Why did she care so much about how she looked to Jack? He was, after all, just a friend. *Right?*

She saw Jack's car turn the corner from her bedroom window and nearly tumbled down the stairs in her hurry to descend. It was important, for some reason, to appear casual when he arrived.

Ha! Nothing like honesty.

She tried to calm her breathing and wished she could rein in her thundering heart as she stood behind the front door. He knocked; she exhaled slowly. With irony she remembered the non-kiss at this very door. One more deep breath and she pulled it open.

"Hi. Am I late?" he asked, but did not wait for an answer, instead handing her a small bouquet of wildflowers.

"Why, thank you. How lovely," she answered softly, still struggling with breathlessness. "That was sweet of you."

Maddie stepped aside and Jack strode into the house, turning toward the kitchen. She followed him and retrieved a crystal vase from the cabinet for the flowers.

"Jack," she began as she filled the vase with water, "I need to tell you something. About last weekend, at your house…"

"It's forgotten."

"No, I really need to tell you. I…wasn't truthful with you, and I know that it's really important to be honest. When I said I wasn't worried about what happened with Ray, I lied. I was really rattled. I'm sorry."

"I knew you were. It was bad timing for both of us. Forget about it. Has he bothered you anymore?"

"No. Not…like that. But anyway, I'm not worrying about him anymore."

"Good. Now, I have a confession too. I also lied."

Maddie put the vase on the table and turned to face Jack, her hands involuntarily clenched behind her back.

Jack approached her and looked her straight in the eyes. "I don't really like sweet and sour chicken."

Before she could protest his joke, he turned and went in search of a soft drink. Maddie smirked. "I want to know, did Todd put you up to this? Did he call you again?"

"Nope. I called him, I mean, I called *you*, and he explained where you were and said he felt crappy that he wasn't going to be here."

"He said *crappy?"*

"Well, not exactly, just bad, you know, so I decided I'd fill in."

So Jack had called her. Maddie beamed inwardly as she dished out the Chinese food.

Jack leaned over her to sample her moo shu pork.

"Yumm. Mmm, I almost forgot. I brought a couple of DVDs." He skipped out to his car and returned a moment later with the two disks. One, a classic, the other a new release, both adventure-romance. Maddie's favorite.

"Did Todd also tell you what kind of bubble bath I use?" Her tone only hinted at sarcasm.

"No, but I'd love to know." He refilled her glass and arranging the silverware, his smile turning into a frown. "Hey, you don't think Todd and I set this up? Maddie, he doesn't even know I'm here. He only made the comment about the food because he felt bad; he was really just talking to himself. The movies were my idea." He grasped her arm. "Honest."

She stopped and peered into his eyes. She felt drawn into them, their depth unknown, but a spreading comfort surrounded her. It was a long moment. "I believe you."

He softened his grip, sliding his hand down her arm to her wrist.

"Good. Maddie, I forced myself to wait until tonight to call you. I knew you needed some time."

She only nodded.

They made quick work of the Chinese dinner and together cleared up the debris. While rinsing plates at the sink, Jack thought again of Ray Tyler. Ray must have stood here. Ray ate at this table, how many years? Ray, *Maddie's husband.*

He took a moment to look at the calendar. The dates

and locations of Ray's "climbs" were written here, along with Todd's dental appointment and important school dates.

"Jack," Maddie began, looking at him from across the room. "Ray's apparently been having an affair."

Jack spun around, a deep frown creasing his face. "What?"

Maddie nodded, looking past Jack out the kitchen window, as if she expected to see Ray striding up the driveway any minute. "It's true. With a friend." She related the story about the travel agent's call and her relationship with Elise Hansen.

Jack shook his head but said little. His face wore a mask of both sympathy and disgust. "I don't know what to say. That's got to be the worst." He cut his words short, wary of upsetting Maddie further.

"I just wanted you to know. We don't need to talk about it," she said. "Let's watch those movies, okay?"

They sat on the couch. Maddie was uncomfortable, at first, not sure how close to sit. Fleetingly, she wondered about Jack's intentions, his expectations. Would he again try to break into her private thoughts, get her to share her jumbled emotions? Her honesty, as he'd put it?

But, no. Jack sank back into the corner of the sofa, his arms crossed on his chest, looking at ease and as natural as if it were his own couch in his own home. Soon, the film engaged them, and they fell into a comfortable quiet.

The film's ending was traditional if not somewhat trite, with the hero embracing his lady before a postcard sunset. Maddie sensed that Jack wanted to comment, but she could only remain stone-faced, her eyes transfixed on the screen.

"Hey, hey…what's the matter? It wasn't *that* sad…" Jack's words, which Maddie knew were meant to console, only increased her melancholy.

"I'm sorry, I can't help it. Life isn't like that. It's-it's not fair…why do they even make movies like that?"

"No, life isn't like that, exactly…sometimes it's worse, sometimes it's better." Jack put his arms around her and drew her closer, patting her back as if she were a child. "C'mon. Let's see a smile."

"I'm sorry." Maddie pulled away from him. She would not, *could not* let Jack get too close. Clearing her throat, she got up and left the room.

"It was only a movie, for God's sake," Jack called after her.

Unable to stop, Maddie steeled herself against the sound of his exasperated sigh.

When she returned, her face washed and her makeup repaired, Jack had donned his jacket. Maddie wrung her hands behind her back as she watched Jack re-box the discs. He wouldn't meet her eyes.

"I, uh, need to get home."

"Really?"

"I had a very early day. If you don't mind, we'll catch the second one some other time?"

"Sure." Maddie's heart sank lower. She'd blown it-again.

They walked outside. The moon was bright and wore a shimmering halo; the air was steely cold.

"Do you really have to go?"

"Yes, I do."

Maddie moved between Jack and his car, staring up at him anxiously. Jack exhaled through pursed lips. "Look, Maddie, that day in the park—when? Two, two-and-a-half months ago? Things were different then. You were happily married, or so I thought. I was in a tailspin. My break up with

Kelly was really bad. But, partly because of you, I've moved past it. I'm ready for something new. Now, *you're* spinning out."

Maddie didn't speak, so he continued.

"Don't-don't misunderstand. You need this time; you're entitled to grieve and to feel sorry for yourself. I know that." He squeezed her shoulders in a small show of support. "And I can't fix it, I can't make it go away. I can't undo what Ray did, and I wouldn't anyway. Ray's not a good person. If it hadn't happened now, it would have eventually.

"But at the same time, I can't keep going this way. I want to be something more to you. Being in Ray's shadow sort of reduces me to the role of your crying towel. And believe me, I have a lot more to offer." He paused to rub her arms gently, and then dropped his hands to her waist.

"I *can* give you a reminder…" He paused, searching for a better word. "A *sample*, of what it could be, *should* be like…" Slipping one hand around the small of her back, the other slid easily into her hair and cupped the back of her head as he drew her body against his. His lips, hesitant at first, were gentle and seeking, then found comfort and purpose. His kiss became confident and full of promise, startling Maddie's senses beyond her expectations. And just when she thought she would fall into some widening abyss of debilitating rapture, he stopped.

He didn't pull away at first. His lips remained pressed softly against hers and she could feel his ragged breathing upon her cheek. It was a moment to hold onto forever. The passion Jack showed her, the brief vision of true emotion and conviction touched a part of her, a memory long ago hidden from consciousness. Unleashed, she knew she could not easily lock it up again.

Jack cleared his throat, his discomfort obvious.

"I have to go." Turning away from her, he fumbled for his keys, dropping them on the driveway. He bent to retrieve them, rising slowly and lifting his eyes to the sky, where the over-full moon hung heavy above them.

"Are you okay?" Maddie asked, her voice barely a whisper.

"Yeah. I just…bumped my head, that's all." He touched the top of his head and grimaced, still staring at the sky.

"On the moon?"

"Something like that."

Maddie had an overwhelming urge to stop him, to prevent him from leaving somehow. But she was frozen to the spot, paralyzed with an enormous, unreasonable fear. Afraid to let him go, terrified to let him stay.

He got into the car and reached for her hand through the window.

"Go inside. You're cold."

"No, I'm not." A brief, forced smile broke through her tight lips over the admission.

"I'll call you." His words echoed a hollow sound. Would he really? Some buried instinct told Maddie she might never hear from him again.

Maddie sat alone in her room. Was Jack right, was she wallowing too deeply in her loss? And was it a loss, really? How long had it been since she'd said, "I love you," to Ray and meant it? Or said it at all?

Questions plagued her. She had been afraid to let herself think about it, but she now realized she really expected Jack to stay. After all, Todd was away for the night. It would have been so easy. Maybe too easy for Jack.

Lying in bed, staring up at nothing, Maddie brooded.

She wished desperately that she could talk to Papa.

Seven

Tuesday morning Maddie managed to catch her boss alone in his office.

"Got a minute?" she asked, trying to sound casual as she peeked around Paul Adams' office door.

"Sure Maddie, come in. What can I do for you?"

Paul was fifty-ish, with a stern face and a kindly demeanor, sometimes an asset in the courtroom.

"I don't know if you've been, uh, privy to any of the office gossip lately, but…" Maddie took a seat in a massive leather chair across from Paul's desk.

Paul leaned forward. "Yes. I heard the news. Maddie, I'm awfully sorry. I've been meaning to talk to you about it, but wasn't sure you were ready."

"Well, as you might imagine, I'm in need of some professional advice."

"You've been with me a long time. I'd be offended if you went to anyone else. Now. The first thing I need to know is, do you still care about Raymond Tyler?"

Almost methodically, Maddie went about the business of filing for divorce. Even though she didn't discuss the matter with Todd, he seemed to know what she was doing and treated her with added affection and care. She was particularly nervous when the initial dissolution papers were filed. Even though she knew Ray was most likely still in Europe, the formality of her actions increased her anxiety. She was really going through with it.

The more she thought about Ray and Elise pounding pitons together, the less uncertain and the angrier she became. And another thought crept into her mind, most often after midnight as she stared into the darkness of her silent bedroom: how long? How long had it been going on without her knowing?

During daylight hours she convinced herself that it didn't matter. Not now, not ever. She couldn't hang on to that kind of anger, it would be neither productive nor healthy. She had Todd to think of, and right now, how she was going to support him. At least the house was hers. She already owned it when she and Ray met. She made a decent salary, and could probably provide the basics. It would be an adjustment, though, living without the generous, if sporadic, paychecks Ray brought home. Todd's extracurricular sports, his science club, his clothes and entertainment would be a stretch; but even if he'd adopted Todd, she wouldn't consider asking Ray for child support.

It made her weary to think about it.

"Your one o'clock is here, Mr. Adams," the intercom on his desk informed Paul as he was browsing through Maddie's case file. Sighing, he closed the folder and slid it to the side.

"Send him in."

Paul stood to greet his new client. Jack McKenzie was a fine looking young man.

"Please, Jack, sit down. Let's see. This is about a custody issue?"

"Yes. I'll get right to the point, Paul. I had a relationship with a young woman and we had a child out of wedlock. I love my son and want to spend time with him, be a part of his life as he's growing up. Kelly, his mother, is making it very difficult for me."

"So I take it you're no longer with this lady, and you never married her, is that correct?"

"Yes, sir. That's correct."

"Did you offer to marry her?"

"Does that matter?" Jack asked, shifting in his chair.

"Not particularly. It just gives me a clearer picture of the situation."

Jack nodded. "Yeah, I offered. She wasn't interested."

"And you're sure the child is yours."

Jack's discomfort grew as the interview with Paul Adams progressed. He was a moral person, he believed, raised to be a decent, responsible adult. Yet he had engaged in unprotected sex with a woman he now disliked. Despised. And that union had produced a child, a boy so innocent and pure, so unaware of the complications his creation had presented to his parents.

Jack squirmed more, unconsciously running fingers through his hair. "Can I *be* sure he's mine? She says he is. People say he looks like me," and at this Jack briefly grinned, "but to me, all babies kinda look alike."

"I'm with you on that. My wife can look at a baby picture for two seconds and say definitively which daughter it is—we have four—and exactly where and when it was taken." Paul shook his head, chuckling. He waved his arm toward the large wall unit behind him, fully loaded with photos of smiling girls.

Jack's smile dimmed. He had only one photo of his son.

"Is this lady now attached to anyone else? A live-in, boyfriend?"

"Not to my knowledge."

"Who cares for the child? I assume she works."

"Her mother."

"What type of home does she provide?"

"I'm sorry?" Jack frowned.

"Do they live in an apartment, a house, a trailer? Is there a yard?"

"Oh, oh, yeah. Uh, she lives in a condo. But her mom lives in a big house not far away. Duncan, my son, spends a lot of time there."

Paul nodded slowly, jotting some notes onto a yellow pad.

"Now. What about your situation? Do you have flexible hours, are you independently wealthy?"

Jack had to smile. "I wish," he responded. He'd made a ton of money last year and spent most of it on Kelly, and the townhouse she convinced him to buy. The townhouse he now hated.

"If you were to care for your son, how would you do it? Would you employ a nanny?"

"I don't know that yet. I haven't thought that far."

Paul nodded again. "That's okay. But these are things you'll have to think about." He scribbled more words, and then sighed. "Well, you got to the point, so I will too. The way I see it, there are three factors we will be looking at. One, what kind of a mother she is. You say her name is Kelly? Can we find her abusive, negligent? Can we attack her way of life, her circle of friends, the environment she provides? Does she endanger the child in any way?

"Next, we would focus on what you have to offer. Can you get yourself into a position to care for a young child? Do you have a female relative, like she does, willing to help you out? Do you have a safe home, a place for your son to play?"

Jack took a deep breath. Nothing Paul said was surprising or encouraging. He had just hoped for something more.

"And last. At some point, you will most likely have to prove paternity."

"Really?" Jack grimaced. "Does it hurt?"

Paul chuckled. "For some, yes, the results hurt. The test is a simple blood test."

Jack stood.

"Okay. So what you're saying is, I catch her doing crack, I get married and buy a house with a big yard, and I can have my son. If, God willing, he is my son."

"It's not quite that cut and dried, Jack, but yes." Paul now stood also, adjusting his waistband over his portly physique. "Say, I understand you're a friend of Maddie's."

Jack was less than enthusiastic with his simple reply. "Yeah. We're friends."

"She's a wonderful person. Seems like I've known Maddie all her life. Going through some tough times right now."

"Yeah, I know." Jack nodded, not meeting Paul's eyes. "Paul, I appreciate your time. I'll be in touch. Thanks again."

Jack left the office feeling defeated. Getting custody of Duncan wasn't looking good. He stopped at the reception desk and pulled out his checkbook.

"Oh, we'll bill you, Mr. McKenzie."

Jack smiled. "Thank you. Hey, would you happen to know if Madelyn Tyler is here today?"

"Maddie? Sure she's here. She works down the hall in our east wing. You want me to ring her?"

"No, that's okay. I'll catch up with her later."

Jack stepped into the hall and waited for the elevator. Somehow, he knew it was Maddie who would step out when the doors opened.

"Oh, Jack!" she said in surprise. "What are you doing here?" *Coming to take me to lunch?*

"I, uh, had an appointment with Paul Adams."

"Oh." Maddie waited, but Jack didn't say more. To her eyes, he looked tired; his hair was not combed and his eyes seemed distant. "Well. How's everything?" She tried to sound upbeat but only succeeded in feeling stupid.

Jack shrugged. "So-so. You?"

"Nothing new. Except I've, uh…" Maddie spoke the words softly. "I've filed for divorce."

A tiny light seemed to appear in Jack's eyes and he lifted his brows slightly, yet his tone was non-committal. "Oh, yeah?"

Maddie nodded. "It's time," she said, looking away.

"Well, that's a step in the right direction, I guess." Still guarded, Jack pressed the elevator button.

Maddie felt a mild sense of panic.

"Todd misses you," she blurted out, a rosy blush filling her cheeks. "Why don't you stop by later? He'd love to show you his new medal."

The elevator doors opened, Jack stepped inside and turned around, holding the doors open with his hand.

"Sorry, I've got a game. I promised the guys. But tell Todd I said hi. Take care, Maddie."

Maddie walked weakly back to her office and sat down. Apparently, Jack wasn't as happy about her news as she thought he would be, wasn't as happy to see her as she was him.

"Who was that guy you were talking to in the hall?"

Della was standing at her door. "Hey kid, you look pale."

"I'm fine. Just tired."

"Well, whoever he was, he sure is cute."

"Cute?" Maddie asked, looking up.

"Let's just say he's a walking testimonial for Levi Strauss. I wouldn't mind gettin' a little piece of *his* action..." Della grinned. Maddie sighed.

"He's just a friend," Maddie said, more to herself than Della. And as she did so many days of late, she skipped her lunch and pushed on with her research.

Her mind wandered, replaying the scene with Jack again and again. She wondered why he was seeing Paul. She wondered what game he was talking about. Most importantly, she wondered if he'd given up on her. As the afternoon progressed, her instincts took over.

"I'm a researcher, darn it. This should be easy." She picked up the phone and called Todd at home. "Did Jack ever mention to you about being on any kind of team?"

"Huh?"

"Todd, put down the game controller. *Listen-to-me.* Does Jack play on any kind of sports team?"

"Of course he does, Mom. Don't be dumb. He even *practices* with the Kings."

Of course he does, Mom. Get a grip. Don't be dumb! "What rink?"

"Ice-O-Dome." Todd paused to absorb the conversation. "Are you going to Ice-O-Dome? I wanna go, too!"

"Not this time."

Maddie stopped at home to change into leggings and a sweater, then headed out for the ice rink.

The atmosphere was decidedly male. *Does testosterone*

have a distinct scent, she wondered, wrinkling her nose at traces of after shave and Lysol mingled with the pervasive odor of perspiration. At least the air was cold. On the ice, a game was in progress, and Maddie wandered in the general direction of the bleachers where a couple of dozen people were alternately cheering and jeering. She sat and watched.

The electronic scoreboard hanging above the far end of the rink counted off the minutes and seconds left in the game. As far as she could tell, it was the red guys against the green guys, and they all looked huge and foreboding. Surely none of these giants could be Jack. The green guys seemed to be all over the ice, surrounding the reds, sticks swinging and swiping. Maddie made a quick count.

"That's not fair," she said aloud.

"What's not fair?" the woman beside her answered, leaning over.

"There are only four red guys. The greens have five!"

The woman grimaced. "We got a penalty. The Rogues are on the *power play,* so we have one less man."

"Oh." Maddie nodded, desperately wishing she'd paid more attention to Todd's endless stream of hockey trivia.

The announcer's voice thundered across the rink, startling Maddie so that she visibly jumped.

"Bulldogs back at full strength."

From out of nowhere, a fifth player in a red jersey skated onto the ice. The woman leaned over again. "Good thing they put Jack back in. He's the only one scoring tonight."

Maddie squinted hard at the players, her interest aroused by the woman's comment. The player now hustling toward the net, his stick deftly swaying back and forth as it pushed the puck steadily along, had the name "MCKENZIE" spelled out between his shoulders. And when he was within range, Jack slammed the puck into the net with such power that Maddie was completely awestruck.

The fans were on their feet, and it was a moment before Maddie was composed enough to stand herself, screaming and squealing with delight, clapping her hands even after most of the others had ceased.

The voice on the loud speaker boomed.

"Bulldogs goal by number 10, McKenzie, unassisted." A pause, then *"That's a hat trick for McKenzie."*

Hat trick? Maddie looked to her would-be educator, and the woman smiled sympathetically.

"First time here?" At Maddie's shy nod, the woman continued. "I'm Deb. I'm the 'team mom'," she said with an immediate laugh. "A hat trick is when one player scores three goals in a game. The score is tied now, and they have a minute to go."

Maddie was immensely grateful for the information. She struggled to locate Jack, but was unable to identify him on the ice. Only a minute left! But the way the refs kept stopping the clock, that minute could take fifteen, Maddie thought.

Watching closely, she finally realized that the players rotated in and out of play, taking turns to rest on the bench behind the rink. With twenty seconds left to play, Jack was back in the game.

"He's very good, isn't he?" Maddie asked Deb, who grinned at her.

"He's the best. In a pissy mood tonight, though. Thankfully, it doesn't hurt his game."

So his bad mood had continued. Maddie sighed. Perhaps she should leave before he saw her. She was contemplating that very thought when a red flash skated by the glass right in front of her, a scarlet blur on the ice traveling at light speed. The Rogue goaltender never saw it coming as the puck rocketed past and tore into the net behind him, a second before the sound of the final buzzer ripped through the arena. Jack's stick was in the air, victorious, and the game was over.

Maddie watched as the team lined up to congratulate their opposition, a long-standing hockey tradition—according to her informer—and one that impressed her. No, she would not leave. She would make sure that Jack knew she had seen him play, cheered him on and applauded his win.

It didn't take long for Jack to notice her there, standing beside the wall as the players filed off the ice and toward the locker room. He tossed his helmet and stick to the floor, and, cocking his head to one side, stared at her in wonder and disbelief.

"Great game," she said, watching his face in hopes of at least a small smile. "You were awesome. Nice *hat treat*."

The grin broke.

"What the hell are you doing here?" he asked, pulling off his gloves and depositing them with the helmet. "Checking up on me?" He reached around her for a quick embrace.

"Maybe," she said, relishing the feel of his arm wrapped around her shoulders for the brief moment he held her. Very brief.

"Sorry, I'm..." Jack shrugged, referring to the sweat pouring off his face, his hair hanging wet and plastered to his skin, his cheeks flushed with color.

He walked her to where the team members were digging bottles of water out of Deb's ice chest and grabbed one for himself.

"Do you like to skate?" he asked suddenly between gulps of cold water.

"I've never tried."

Jack's eyes opened wide in surprise. "Impossible," he told her. He took another draught of the water, and then poured the little that was left onto his already dripping head and face. "Come on."

Practically dragging Maddie to the front counter, Jack leaned over to talk to the desk clerk conspiratorially, gratefully drying his face with the towel she offered him. The din inside the building made it difficult for Maddie to hear his words, but soon he turned and asked her what size shoe she wore.

"Six, why?"

Before she knew what was happening, Jack had her on the bench and was fitting her with a pair of ice skates.

"Jack, I don't think I can."

"Hey, you've skied, right? Roller skated?"

"Sure, but—"

"Come on." He took her hand and she tried to stand on the skates.

"But aren't you exhausted? You just came off!"

"I'm still wired." Jack looked over his shoulder as he led her to the rink gate. "Terri! Give me ten minutes, 'kay?"

The girl behind the counter nodded, calling back, "Ten minutes 'til *Zamboni* is on the ice."

The rink was empty. Around the outside, people waited, putting on skates and gloves in preparation for the open skating hour that would begin soon.

"Okay. We'll take this real easy." Jack took her hands, pulling her toward him onto the ice, skating slowly backwards. "Just go with me."

Maddie trembled inside; she was unsure if it was her fear of skating or the feel of Jack's hands grasping hers that brought on the tremors, her legs awkwardly stiff and uncooperative as he pulled her along.

"Aren't you afraid you'll bump into something?" she asked, feeling both stupid and clumsy under his gaze.

Jack smiled. "See anything behind me?"

Of course, the rink was clear and large, and of course, Jack knew exactly where he was.

"Try skating," he suggested. "Pretend you're on wheels."

Maddie complied, alternately moving her feet outward in a skating motion until she managed a rudimentary rhythm of her own. Jack seemed pleased and moved to her side, holding only one hand as they continued to circle the rink together. A group of young teenage girls had gathered at the glass, and they smiled and waved at Jack each time he passed.

"You're doing great," Jack told Maddie as he finally moved behind her. "You just keep going. I'm right behind you." He held her lightly by the hips for a few moments, and then let go of her.

"Jack! Come back," she called in panic. But he was, indeed, right behind her, and quickly grasped her shoulders in an effort to calm her fear.

They stopped moving. Jack squeezed her arms, leaning down to speak directly into her ear.

"You can do this. I want you to skate alone around the rest of the way."

"No, I'm scared."

"Trust me, Maddie. You've got to trust me. I'll be right behind you."

"What if I fall?" Memories of Ray's demands on the slopes threatened her confidence.

"I can skate faster than you can fall," Jack whispered, and Maddie closed her eyes against the shiver that enveloped her body. He gave her a little push and she began to skate, dreading the moment he would let go. And eventually, he did let go, hanging back to give her room to skate ahead.

The girls at the window were rapt, whispering and giggling quietly as they watched their hero skate with his new girlfriend. Even some of his teammates stopped near the locker room door to watch the arena and the attention Jack paid the pretty girl in the pink sweater.

Maddie could barely breathe.

God, I have to do this. Trust Jack. Don't let me fall!

Slowly, carefully, Maddie took the curve at the far end of the oval rink, concentrating on looking smooth and capable. She didn't dare wonder if Jack was still behind her, or how far away he was. She kept her eyes on the exit door. She was doing fine until the sound of an engine, a loud roar akin to that of a giant lawnmower, filled the rink and startled Maddie from her ice exhibition. Abruptly she turned her head in the direction of the sound, and the break in concentration disrupted her momentum, throwing her off-balance.

Instantly she looked down at her skates, trying to get back into rhythm, but it was too late. She tried to remember how to drag the toe of her skate to brake, and in doing so made herself even more insecure. Terror filled her head. *Oh no, I'm going down!*

The thought did not even fully cross her mind and Jack was with her, his arms not merely grasping her waist but wrapped fully around her, the heat of his chest warming her back and shoulders. Looking forward, Maddie realized they were only a few feet away from the rink door.

They slowed to a stop, but still he held her, his lips close to her ear.

"Now, is there anything more I can do to earn your trust?" he whispered before kissing her neck briefly. He waited patiently for her to catch her breath, to calm down from her scare.

Maddie closed her eyes. Jack's show of affection was not lost on her, but she hesitated to acknowledge it for fear that she was over-reacting. Perhaps it was only in sympathy, a consolation for her pathetic performance. Taking a deep breath, she mentally forced aside the exhilarating feel of his lips against her skin. But she could not begin to slow the wild flutter in her chest.

"Just tell me, who is Sam Bony, and what is that awful noise?"

He was still laughing at her as he helped her remove the skates. Behind him, the Zamboni ice machine plowed around the rink, resurfacing the ice for the impatient skaters lined up around the perimeter.

Maddie hovered near the door while Jack gathered up his discarded gear. She pretended not to watch as several of his teammates crowded around him, some of them glancing her way as they talked, their voices lost in the sound of the rock music entertaining the skaters. Finally, Jack approached her.

"Was that fun, or what?" he asked, leaning casually on his hockey stick.

Maddie smiled, her eyebrows lifting in a "maybe" gesture. Timidly, she chose her words carefully, trying to sound casual and non-committal.

"If you want to come by, I have some leftover sweet and sour chicken," she offered.

Jack looked down, then back toward his friends who seemed to be waiting. "Thanks. I, uh, think I'd better go with the guys, they have this little victory celebration planned, you know, tonight we pretty much cinched first place, and…"

"Sure. You can't miss that." Maddie turned to go. "Thanks for the lesson," she called over her shoulder.

"Maddie." Jack reached for her arm before she could get completely out the door. She turned, expectant, feeling herself begin to drown in the depths of his eyes. He stared at her for several moments, his fingers working into the palm of her hand. Finally finding a voice, he nodded at her. "Thanks for coming."

Eight

Maddie thought he might call her the next day, or the day after that, but Jack was incommunicado during the week that followed their escapade on the ice. Doubts about his feelings, her new single life, and the future clouded her thoughts, although she tried to keep up a cheerful attitude to her co-workers and her son.

The days flew and they dragged; no day seemed much different than another. During a particularly dismal afternoon of worry and anxiety, Maddie took note of the calendar on her desk. A date stood out, circled with red marker by a young boy sitting at his mother's work desk on a weekend long ago, a boy who would be twelve years old in five days.

"Great," she whispered, running both hands through her hair. "How could I have forgotten?" Unconsciously she brought her fingers to her mouth, but her fingernails were already bitten so short there was nothing left to bite.

What can I do, what can I do? She wanted, no, *needed,* to do something special for Todd's birthday. Something to brighten up their lives, something to look forward to and happily back on afterward.

She started when her phone rang at 3:30 p.m. Todd was home from school.

"Hi honey. Hey, I was wondering if you had any plans

for Friday night?"

"Well, gee, Mom, I don't know..." Todd giggled. Maddie could hear him digging around in a bag of chips or crackers. "How about you?"

"Well, I was thinking about heading down to the marina, you know that great restaurant you love down there? With calamari, mahi-mahi..."

"Awesome! That'd be so sick, Mom! Can we really?"

"Sick? Um, sure. If that's what you'd like to do."

"Can I bring a friend?"

"Of course. Bryan is welcome to come."

"Uhhh..."

"What is it, honey?"

"I wasn't talking about Bryan." More munching. Maddie waited.

"Well? Who then? David? Chad?"

"Jack."

Jack. Just the sound of his name and Maddie swore her play-dough heart squeezed into a different shape.

"Gee, Todd, I don't know. Jack may be busy."

"Can we at least ask him, Mom?"

"Well, sure. Of course."

It took every ounce of courage she had left that afternoon, but after five trips to the coffee room, three sharpened pencils and one antacid, Maddie dialed Jack's number.

"McKenzie."

"Jack? Hi. It's Maddie."

"Hi. Wow. It's good to hear your voice. To what do I owe the honor?"

"Well, I have a little proposition for you. Friday is Todd's birthday, and, well..." Maddie paused to swallow, hoping he hadn't heard the tiny quiver to her voice. "I'm taking him down to the Whaler for dinner and I thought you might like to join us." There. She'd said it.

"Friday night, huh? Hmm." He seemed hesitant.

"We'll understand if you can't make it. It's short notice, I know."

After what seemed like an eternity, Jack replied.

"I wouldn't miss it for the world. Can I pick you guys up? Say, seven o'clock?"

"You don't have to."

"I insist. You tell Todd to be ready. We'll show him a good time. And maybe his friend, what's his name? Brad? Maybe he'd like to come too. A foursome."

"Are you sure?"

"Absolutely." Jack was smiling, and Maddie could hear it. "I look forward to seeing you," he added, his voice softer now.

"Me too."

Maddie hung up feeling better than she had in weeks.

Friday afternoon found both Maddie and Todd excitedly preparing for their big date. Jack had called Todd after school to confirm the time, and Todd could hardly contain himself. Maddie watched him thoughtfully from the bedroom door as Todd carefully combed his hair before the mirror.

"Jack says he has a surprise for us, Mom. I wonder what it is."

"No idea…"

"He's so cool, Mom."

"I know, honey."

By seven Todd was pacing the kitchen, wearing his best clothes. Maddie's own stomach seemed knotted. She paced too, not as noticeably as she pretended to tidy up the kitchen. She'd chosen a long, crinkled black dress with a pink rose pattern and black lace inset in the front. A black velvet ribbon adorned her newly curled hair.

"Mom, look!"

Maddie hurried to join Todd at the kitchen window to watch as a long, black limousine turned into the driveway.

"Wow! That's the surprise!" Todd bounded out the door, nearly colliding with Jack as he came up on the porch. Maddie laughed at the sight, her anticipation high, her nervousness fading. Jack looked handsome and solid. She'd missed him enormously.

He bent to give her a brief kiss on the cheek. "I see everybody's ready. You look lovely."

"Thanks," she said. She knew she was blushing and would stammer if she said anything more. Quickly she grabbed her purse and they were on their way to pick up Bryan.

Jack had made reservations and they were seated at the water's edge. Outdoor gas heaters warmed the area around their table, and the boys kept the talk lively and comical. Todd was riding a wave of adolescent exuberance and Maddie hid many smiles.

"And guess what else? We get to go on a camping trip!" Todd told Jack, who nodded, his face mimicking Todd's enthusiastic one. "The campground is near the beach. We get to barbeque stuff, and—"

"And even the principal's coming!" Bryan said, clearly stunned that the head man from school would consider hanging out with a bunch of sixth-graders.

"Yeah, but we can bring our own MP3s and stuff."

"And who is going along? Besides the teachers and

principal?" Maddie wanted to know.

"My folks signed up to help out," Bryan said. "My dad usually works on weekends, but he 'specially took that weekend off. They said Todd could come with *us*."

"Oh," Maddie said softly. It was obvious to Maddie that Bryan's folks were aware of her new status as a single parent, a fact that she'd rather forget.

"Sounds like fun. You say it's at the beach?" Jack asked.

"Yeah. With campfires and everything. It's going to be so cool," Todd said with finality. "I can't wait."

Jack looked thoughtful, watching Todd's youthful enthusiasm with what Maddie decided was a subtle longing. His expression touched her.

Suddenly, Jack reached into the inside breast pocket of his jacket and withdrew an envelope. "I almost forgot. This is for you."

Todd lifted the flap with great ceremony, and pulled out the gift certificate from the Ice-O-Dome pro shop. Holding it close to the flickering light from the candle on the table, he gasped, his eyes large with surprise and delight.

"Wow! Is this for *everything*? Thanks, Jack!" He thrust the slip before his mother's face in excitement. "Mom, look, I'm gonna play ice hockey!"

Maddie looked quickly at Jack, mildly chastising him for the expense; the certificate included full ice hockey gear and lessons. Although no amount was designated, it had to be worth close to a thousand dollars.

Jack shrugged. "I'm a stockholder. I practically own the place."

Dinner was finished all too soon, and Jack picked up the tab.

"Jack, you shouldn't. We invited you."

"It's my pleasure. I was thrilled to be invited."

Maddie sighed and shook her head. They left the restaurant, and the boys immediately spotted a video game arcade nearby on the boardwalk.

After Jack argued in Todd's favor, Maddie relented and allowed the boys to go in alone, each grasping a five-dollar bill.

"Make it last," Jack called after them, and Todd glanced back with a nod.

Maddie looked out across the harbor. The air was warmer than she expected, and several boats were just returning from a sunset tour, their small cabins dimly lit. She started to comment on how pretty it all looked, then decided it would sound too cliché. Instead, she sighed.

"Pretty, isn't it?" Jack said, standing behind her. Maddie could not resist a giggle.

"What's so funny?"

"Nothing. Just that…" she laughed again. "I was just going to say that."

He murmured something about great minds and leaned against the wooden rail before them. Silence fell between them as they watched the boats progress inland.

Unable to help herself, Maddie stole a look at Jack. The breeze lifted his hair a little and his expression was pensive.

"What are you thinking about?" she asked softly.

"I was really a jerk when I saw you at the office."

Maddie didn't say anything, remembering the pain she felt that afternoon.

"I'd just gotten some bad news. It was wrong of me to be so rude." He paused, then, "I was shocked to see you at the rink. What made you decide to track me down?"

Maddie shrugged, embarrassed, unable to tell him the

truth. But there was no suitable lie, either, so she didn't answer.

"Came to chew me out, didn't you?" Now he grinned. "I figured if I got you onto skates, you'd forget about my bad manners."

He'd been right. On the ice, all other thoughts were banished. There was only Jack, Jack's hands on her body; the ice, the blades cutting cleanly through the surface; the fear, the somehow arousing fear of losing her balance, of losing her sanity, of losing Jack's faith in her.

"Well, whatever. I'm glad you came. I've been thinking about you a lot. Wishing I knew more about you."

"Oh. Well… Let's see," she began, almost coyly as she, too, leaned against the rail. "You already know where I'm from, that I went to Delaney High and graduated two years after you. My middle name is Marie and I majored in English." She paused to look briefly into his eyes. *Trust me*, they said.

"Go on."

"When I was sixteen, I fell in love with my French tutor."

"How sweet." His comment, however trite and possibly sarcastic, did not match the look in his eyes. *Tell me. Tell me everything.*

Maddie took a deep breath before continuing. *You want it all? Here goes.*

"When I was eighteen, I followed him to France."

At this revelation Jack started and stared openly at Maddie. "What?"

"His name was Thomas LaForge and I was crazy, mad in love with him. And he loved me, and we shacked up together. He was twenty-eight years old."

Jack's eyes were wide with unabashed surprise. "But I

thought…"

"I know, I know. I misled you, I guess, that day in the park. It's not something I generally bring up, you know? I wanted to tell you, to fill in the details of those early years…but the time never seemed right. I'm sorry."

Jack digested the news. "Then where does old Ray fit in? What happened to your first-uh, Thomas?"

Maddie took a moment to compose her words. Drawing another deep breath, she turned to face Jack. "Tom was a naturalist, a...a Bohemian sort. Kind of a scholar, too. He was an accomplished writer, teacher, also a sailor. In fact, he kept a boat down here, after we moved back to America. Over there somewhere." She pointed out into the black waters.

"Thirteen years ago, Tom found out he had cancer. He was devastated. He started treatments, but it was unclear if it was helping or not. One Sunday he went sailing, alone, and sailed right into a squall. He didn't come back." Her voice had become almost monotonic, her eyes seeing something long ago passed. "There was talk, of course, of suicide. I never believed it."

"God, Maddie, I'm so sorry," Jack began, shaking his head slowly. "I had no idea."

Deaf to his voice, she continued her tale. "Two days after the funeral, I found out I was pregnant. The following year, my father died, and I was left with an infant, a despondent mother and widow's weeds."

Now Jack was beyond speech, his eyes following her gaze across the harbor, as if trying to see what she saw. "So Todd is…"

"Tom's son. Yes."

"That explains a lot," Jack said softly. "Wow. I am *shocked.*"

"I knew you would be. It's a lot." She paused again to gather her memories together. "After Todd was born, I moved in with my parents. It seems like almost immediately, Daddy became ill. Mother and I took care of him and Todd both. When he died, I knew I had to do something, so I went back to school to study law. Then I met Ray."

"Where did you hook up with him?"

"Tom left me a little money. I used it to make the down payment on my house, but I had payments. Out of the blue, Paul called me up looking for an assistant. He got my name from the community college. I got the job, and Ray was a client of Mr. Stern's at the time. He took me to lunch one day." She smiled briefly. "We were married in six months, I think. I guess you could say it seemed like the right thing to do at the time. But Mom became bitterly depressed. She lived with us for a while, and then we had to put her in a…a home." This last memory was particularly painful for Maddie, and she shuddered slightly.

Jack wrapped an arm around her shoulders and pulled her close for a hug. "I am so sorry. Had I known all that…"

"It's okay."

"Todd must know, huh?"

"Oh yes. I would never have him thinking Ray was his father. Never. Thomas was too good a man, too good a friend. Todd knows all about his father. I'm kind of surprised he didn't tell you himself."

"I think he wanted to. Maybe he felt he would betray you somehow. He's a pretty perceptive kid."

"He's a lot like his father. I think Ray could never get past that. And that's why Todd wasn't upset to see him go. They never really connected." Maddie drew in a deep breath.

Jack only nodded. The boys were coming back.

The limo's headlights lit the front porch as the boys tumbled out of the car and scrambled for the door.

"Get out the cake and ice cream, I'll be right in," Maddie called.

"Thanks again, Jack! I had a great time!" Todd turned back from the porch with a wave.

Jack waved too, then helped Maddie out of the back seat. "Well, here we are again."

"Yeah." She stood before him, every breath a conscious effort to stay calm. "Have I passed your trust and honesty test now?" she asked quietly.

"Passed? My own admissions pale in the face of yours," he said, shaking his head. "And I thank you for sharing. It means everything to me." He toyed with the velvet ribbon in her hair. "Now I'm thinking I'd better try to kiss you goodnight again, only…"

"Oh, only what?" she asked, her anticipation mounting. His nearness and the memory of his last kiss filled her with an urgency she had denied for too long. "What excuse could you possibly have?"

"Only, I bumped my head pretty hard last time," he said, lifting his eyes and smiling at the starry sky.

"Ah, but there's no moon tonight. You're safe." Maddie slipped her arms around his neck, rising on tiptoes to kiss him before he could make another joke and delay further. Behind them, the limo driver turned off his engine and they were in darkness.

"Something tells me I will never be safe around you," he murmured against her lips.

It was the most loving, romantic and sumptuous kiss she could ever remember sharing with anyone in her life. Exquisite. New, and yet not new at all. Maddie's entire body responded in a way that said, "this is a fit. A perfect fit." His lips, warm, moist and hungry, traveled away from her mouth, slowly exploring her cheek and resting in that sweet, hot-key spot just below her ear. Jack sighed; Maddie shuddered in delight.

He pulled back a little, looked into her face, then turned his eyes toward the house.

"My head is okay, but I may need a cold shower," he said, laughing. Greedily, he kissed her again.

Maddie felt a weakness spread throughout her legs and arms as she clung to Jack. But with that weakness, there was strength; strength in knowing that the man who held her so tightly was a man in whom she could trust, and upon whom she could depend. There was nothing—nothing at all—about Jack McKenzie that did not suit her.

His face grew somber, and Maddie wondered about his thoughts as he peered into her eyes, his fingers lightly caressing her face. Her own feelings threatened to overwhelm her, and she fought to remain in the moment; her mind's eye showed Jack carrying her through the door and up the stairs to her bedroom.

Peals of childish laughter drifted toward them from the open front door and the picture dissolved.

"I didn't realize, when I asked to know more about you…" Jack began, his voice a warm caress in the night air.

"You didn't bargain for all that I came up with, did you?"

"I was hoping for favorite color, favorite ice cream, maybe your birthday…" he smiled and again pressed his lips against hers.

"Mmm. Blue, chocolate chip and…gee, I guess my birthday is in two weeks." She fingered the top button on his shirt. "I love roses, and romance novels, and pizza with everything, except anchovies. I love Maroon 5 and Keith

Urban. I love antiques and Depression glass, and I love gardening. And, I love my truck. Anything else you need to know?"

And me, he wanted to know, hoping she could not read his mind…yet. *Can you add me to that list*?

"Just, if you'll let me take you away from here, somewhere fun and beautiful and exciting to celebrate your birthday. Alone," he said.

The implication was clear. Something new started tonight, and Jack McKenzie intended to see it through.

Nine

Maddie squeezed Della Kissinger's arm as she walked by her friend's desk. Della shook her head. "I have never seen you so radiant, girlfriend. And it's only five o'clock and you have three new files in your basket." She followed her co-worker out to the elevator.

"I'm sure I don't know what you're talking about," Maddie said, looking around as if to search for Della's meaning.

"You're humming, for goodness sake. I want whatever it is you're getting."

In the parking garage, Maddie called out to Della. "Let's have lunch tomorrow!"

Della nodded and smiled as Maddie climbed into her pickup, started it up and cranked up a song by Jason Mraz.

"It's Jack, isn't it?" Della called, as Maddie drove past her on the way out.

And so it was with little surprise to the others that on Tuesday morning Maddie was actually late to work. The girls were huddled when she strode by their desks on her way to her office, giggles interspersed with their "good mornings." Inside her office, Maddie discovered why. On her desk was a flower arrangement. Roses, she guessed to be about two dozen, white, pink and red perfectly arranged in a beautiful dark blue vase. The display took her breath away. Spinning around, she found the secretaries crowded just outside her door, craning their necks to watch her reaction. She could only grin at them.

Della Kissinger pushed past them and bent to take a whiff. "He must be one helluva guy."

Maddie quickly found the small card and pulled it from its envelope.

""You left out the color of the roses. Your choice. I cannot wait for our weekend together, anticipation consumes me. Yours, Jack."

Carefully she turned the vase around, feeling the patterned design. "It's cobalt glass," she said softly.

"What?" Della asked, her curiosity brimming.

"Cobalt. It's from the depression era. It's sometimes very valuable, and this kind of piece is really hard to find. I wonder how he did it?"

"A man in love can do anything, honey. Trust me."

Maddie looked up just as Della left the room.

A man in love?

She got nothing more done that morning.

Paul stopped by her office later that afternoon.

"What's this I hear about…oh, nice," he said, viewing the roses and Maddie's beaming face. "These wouldn't be from that nice McKenzie fellow?"

"They might be," she joked. "They just might."

Paul sat down.

"Well Madelyn we've had news from Ray's attorneys. All seems to be in order. No demands, no changes."

"Good. Let's hope it goes smoothly and then just goes away."

"Just curious, Maddie, does Jack know about your first, uh, relationship?"

Had anyone but Paul asked, she would have declined to discuss it. She talked to nobody about Thomas, and she liked it that way.

"Yes. He does. I really like him, Paul, and I wanted to be up front about everything."

"That's good. It only came up for me because in reviewing your file, I didn't want to lose sight of the fact that Thomas left you some money and property; I included a provision that Ray must sign a quitclaim deed on the house. I'm sure Thomas would hate it if this louse took anything from you."

"Did you know Thomas, Paul? He went to Southwestern briefly, you know, before he decided he didn't need to be a biologist. Isn't that where you graduated?"

"Yes, I did, but I didn't really know him. Different fields of study, I was into law enforcement back then."

"Oh, of course. That's right. Well, I appreciate your looking out for me on this." Maddie's eyes came to rest, again, upon the flowers and her face softened.

Paul shook his head whimsically. "He's a nice young man, Maddie. I hope things work out for the two of you."

She thanked him from her romantic haze and he left her office smiling.

She read the card again. "Yours, Jack." Is he really mine?

The card was special, and she reached beneath her desk to retrieve her purse. Jack's little note fit into the small, zippered slot in the side. Before closing up her bag, she noticed a folded piece a paper and withdrew it. The identity report on Todd she'd stashed there days before.

After carefully reviewing the report again, she picked up the phone and called the firm issuing it. She learned, after giving significant personal information, that the bank account had been verified and that she should contact the bank for more explanation.

She wondered briefly if she should ask Paul for advice. If it was for real, who could have done it? Jack? No. For one thing, Jack didn't know Todd went by La Forge. And anyway, he'd never do anything like that without asking her. Of this she was certain.

Her mind wandered back to the year Todd was born. Those dreary days after Thomas' death, when life meant almost nothing and the baby in her arms cried incessantly. She was living with her parents. Her father came to her late one night and took the screaming child from her arms. Little Todd had quieted and gone to sleep.

"Sometimes when a Mama is stressed, the child feels it," he said quietly. He sat with her, rocking the sleeping baby in his arms. He began to hum, then to sing under his breath, an Irish lullaby, many of the words sounding like gibberish to Maddie's Americanized ears.

"I wish," he said at last, "that I could be around ter see this little laddie grow up. I wish I had a little something put terway fer 'im, fer when he's a-grown."

Maddie recalled few intimate moments with her father; a quiet, very private Irishman who'd always wanted a son that never came. In retrospect, Maddie realized he'd already known he was dying that night so long ago.

She didn't think about him often, but when she did she felt a tear come to her eye.

Could this money be the "little something" he had managed to put away for his grandson? If so, why hadn't she found out about it sooner? Maybe this was a mystery not to be solved.

As her birthday weekend approached, Maddie, too, felt anticipation at spending the time with Jack. And with her excitement came fears. She'd been intimate with only two men in her life, not including a couple of one-night-stands during her college years.

It had been a very long time since she'd allowed anyone to even get as close as Jack was now. She had to admit that she shut Ray out long before he'd finally left her. Jack was everything she wanted and more, but she was anxious and doubtful about her abilities as his lover. Every time she imagined joining Jack in bed, she overloaded and her mind went "tilt."

She was going with him, nonetheless. What would happen, would happen.

On the day before they were to leave, a package arrived, addressed to Maddie. Todd was off somewhere with his neighborhood pals. She was packing, nervously flitting about her bedroom when the postman arrived. The large, flat, rectangular package labeled "fragile," bore a Swiss postmark. She signed for it, and carried the package to the living room to open it.

Maddie stripped the brown paper away, revealing a large, beautifully framed oil painting. The hauntingly familiar scene showed a lighthouse on the shore, with a shining, lazy-looking river passing in the distance behind it. She did not recognize the painter's name, but it was decidedly Impressionist, in the style of Claude Monet. Maddie had always loved Monet's work. But who sent it? The package bore no return address. Quickly she re-examined the torn packaging. Not a clue, except that it was mailed in Bern.

Surely not Ray? He *was* in Switzerland.

She lifted the heavy painting and propped it on the mantle above the fireplace. She'd deal with this new mystery when she returned.

Early Saturday morning found Maddie and Jack flying in to Reno, Nevada, and then renting a car to take them to the lake. Tahoe was glistening and clean, and the cabin Jack rented charmed them. A wide, comfortable deck surrounded the front, and a quaint, river rock fireplace lay stocked with logs ready to light. Dumping their suitcases, they got back into the car and drove around, stopping for lunch, window-shopping and to make reservations for a guided hiking adventure in the afternoon.

They went back to the cabin and found it chilly inside. Maddie pulled out the *People* magazine she'd bought, kicked off her shoes, and stretched out on the bed while Jack lit the fire. "I need to text Todd," she murmured.

"I'm sure he and Bryan are not thinking about anything besides *Assassin's Creed* right now."

"Gosh, I hope not. Don't they still play *Sonic*?"

Jack grinned and shook his head. The fire took hold and the logs began to crackle. Jack knelt before it, staring into the growing flames, and Maddie watched him in fascination. Pulling open the drapes, he gazed out at the sea of dark pines and the minuscule view of the lake in the distance. High, puffy, cumulus clouds drifted slowly and silently across the bright blue sky.

"Beautiful. Just beautiful," he murmured, then looked back at Maddie.

She lowered her magazine and watched as Jack's expression changed. She couldn't quite guess at his thoughts, only that they weren't about the outside scenery. He turned then, and pulled the draperies closed again. What little daylight had peeked in, now eclipsed. Standing near the bed, he pulled his sweater over his head and carefully laid it across the back of the chair, his eyes intense on Maddie's. Next, he did the same with his T-shirt.

"Jack," she began, her fingers grasping the magazine a little too tightly.

Jack sat down to untie his sneakers, and then flipped the light switch near the bed to "off."

"Jack," she said again, her voice edged with mock irritation. "What are you doing?"

Still he didn't speak.

"It's only one o'clock."

"So?" he answered with a grin. He undid the top button on his Levi's.

Maddie was suddenly flushed. The sight of Jack standing before her in just his jeans ignited her. It was the first time he had bared his chest in her presence. She felt her stomach contract and her lips go dry. And now he was taking off those jeans.

"Wait." She tossed the magazine to the floor. Crawling off the bed, she stood beside him and slowly pulled her own sweater over her head, tossing it onto the chair with his. Beneath it she wore only a simple fitted camisole with a tie in the front.

She found it hard to speak so she didn't say anything more. The soft, warm light coming from the fire was enough, just enough to cast a luminous glow, flickering and dancing as though the flames were licking at them. Boldly Maddie slipped her fingers into his trousers and began unbuttoning the remaining buttons. It was something she had never done in her life.

She couldn't help the flashing comparisons that

invaded her mind. Ray would never have allowed her to undress him. It was a power thing. Jack's expression confirmed that she was doing the right thing. Soon, Jack was undressing her.

Maddie had never known lovemaking could be like this. Thomas had been, well, routine and subdued. He often worried about "hurting" her. She had worshiped him, and always concerned herself more with his pleasure than her own.

She had learned new moves from Ray. But Ray was moody and self-absorbed, and Maddie had long ago given up feeling anything more than a rather quick thrill.

Now, Jack. Jack was another story. It was clear that her pleasure was his pleasure, and if Maddie had worried about her own performance, her fears were dashed the moment she lay down with him. Now her only fear would be in the knowledge that there could never be anyone else for her again.

She could not get enough of touching Jack. The modesty and hesitation she felt before melted away, and their naked intimacy became the most natural thing in the world. The giving up of her body, her most precious and personal being, was a virginal feeling, the greatest gift she could ever give any man. It was a first for Maddie.

Jack's anticipation overwhelmed him; he tried not to hurry. He wanted everything to be perfect and right between them. But it had been months since the first glimmer of desire glowed between them, months of learning, anxiety, risks…and waiting. Waiting for the time to be right. And now that it was, Jack was hard pressed to take it too slowly.

Maddie was beautiful, beautiful not in just a physical sense, he decided, but beautiful in her simple loving ways.

Here was a woman he found joy in delighting, someone to whom he could demonstrate his love without fear of retribution. She was easy to please. She surprised him with her response to his very touch, and he wanted to touch her everywhere.

When at last they came together in perfect unity, Jack, too, knew it had never been like this before. Maddie held him so tightly he thought they would merge into one. *This could not possibly get any better.*

They clung to one another for some time, their hearts pounding and their bodies slick against each other. Jack at last found her ear with his lips.

"Maddie. There's something I have to tell you."

"Whatever it is, it can't change the way I feel right now," she whispered.

"It could."

"A confession?"

"Yes." He propped his head on one hand, and, grasping her chin with his other, pulled her face toward his. "I've been wanting to tell you this for a while…I wanted to tell you before this happened. It's just…"

"Oh, what, Jack? Please!"

"Just that I love you, with all my heart and all my soul. And I will, ever and always."

Maddie stared at him for a long moment, eyes glistening, and Jack kissed her cheek. Then, lying back, he pushed the hair from his own face and spoke toward the ceiling.

"When I think about how different things would have turned out if…if we had gotten together back then, all this time..."

"Our lives would surely be different, but I wouldn't trade this moment right now for anything," she said, sniffing and climbing on top of him.

They made love again. The urgency gone, his confession made, Jack took the time to enjoy and tantalize the woman he loved more than anything in his life.

They rescheduled their hike and decided to spend the rest of the day in bed, agreeing that nothing could be more fun or exciting. Jack took the opportunity to talk about his past.

"First, there was Carol. We were college roommates, then lovers, then we got married over spring break," Jack recalled for Maddie as they watched the fire mellow into a slow burn. "Carol was always fond of saying how marriage had ruined our friendship. She left me for some neo-hippie from Berkeley. So, I quit school and joined the Air Force."

"Do you keep in touch?"

"Nope. No need." He was hesitant to say too much; old insecurities bubbled up whenever he thought about his ex-wife. "I knocked around a bit in the service, but I basically kept away from anything serious." *Until I met Kelly Mathis. Then things got serious real fast.*

Maddie seemed to be reading his mind. "Where did you meet Kelly?"

"I'm embarrassed to say, it was in a bar. I was lonely, she was looking. It was hot, and brief, and then we sorta broke up. She called me a month later to tell me about Duncan."

And how did *that happen, anyway?* It had been the final straw. He never should have trusted her. He should have taken precautions himself.

Unbidden, Kelly's last words came hauntingly to mind: *"I don't think it's a good idea for Duncan to get attached to you, Jack. In fact, I'm probably moving to New York. You won't be seeing him anyway, so why complicate things? Besides. You don't have room in your life for a child."* It was a blow from which he was still reeling.

Jack shook his head to clear the memories away. He would have to sort it out it later.

Maddie reached from the bed to gain Jack's discarded T-shirt, pulling it over her head and down to her hips.

"What's this?" he wanted to know. "If you're cold, I can remedy that."

"No, not cold. I just like to wear something in bed."

Jack grinned. "Modesty is so passé, babe."

"I'm not being modest," she asserted, her chin high. "Just practical. What if there was an earthquake or something?"

Jack laughed out loud, shaking his head, as Maddie blushed. She toyed with the silver charm that hung from a chain around Jack's neck.

"It's a Celtic knot. My grandmother gave it to me on my fifteenth birthday."

Maddie held the piece in her fingers. It was about the size of a nickel, an intricate design of woven silver strands.

"It's so beautiful, and heavy. Is it old?"

"It was hers as a child. There are several different ones, this one is supposed to represent 'eternal love.' See how smooth it is on the back? I've worn it for twenty-two years."

Maddie nodded, deftly running her fingers over the intricate design. Suddenly, concern crossed her face.

"Twenty-two years! Your birthday-it's..."

"Tomorrow. The day after yours."

Without another word, Jack sat up and pulled the necklace over his head, placing it around Maddie's neck.

"Thank you," she said softly. She turned the charm again, examining it closely. "What does I A M mean? Let's see, I Am, I am what??"

Once again, Jack laughed at her, then kissed her on the nose.

"No, dear heart. It's just 'I.A.M.' Ian Arthur McKenzie." My mother had it engraved on there because she was so sure I'd lose it." And to Maddie's puzzled face, he continued. "*Ian.* It's my name, silly girl. You know, Ian, John…Jack."

Still confused, Maddie shook her head. "Ian. Isn't that Scottish?"

"Yeah. It was my mother's gift to herself. She grew up in the South, but she's a Scot, you know. My pop hated the name from the start, my mother being the only thing he'd ever have to do with the Scots. He refused to call me by my real name, insisting that in America the name was John."

Maddie nodded.

"He got back at her when my brother was born. Insisted on naming him Sean. But of course, the hypocrite couldn't call *him* John, too…" Jack laughed sarcastically.

"So, Sean is *Irish* for John," Maddie murmured.

"Since he wouldn't call me Ian, I wouldn't let him call me John. By 7th grade, I was Jack."

"At least he cared enough to fight with you."

"Now that's a new angle. I'll have to remember that the next time he's reaming me out for one of my many shortcomings."

"Got any more secrets?"

"Well, only that I was once mauled by a bear…" He showed her three long scars that crossed his breast.

She kissed his chest where a startled bear had once defended her cub, and whispered, "I love you, Ian McKenzie."

Ten

Their flight home bumped along on pockets of rough sky. The storm that had brought a late spring rain to the mountain left rocky patches in the air, but neither Maddie nor Jack seemed to notice too much. Sated, content, they held hands and talked softly about everything and nothing.

While digging in her purse for a stick of gum, Maddie's hand closed on a forgotten piece of paper. Pulling it out, she stiffened slightly at the sight of the mysterious identity report Todd received the week before. She handed it to Jack.

"What's this?" He opened it, raised his eyebrows and then looked back at Maddie. "Did you order this?"

She nodded. "In a way, yes. The school has this service where you can find out if anyone is stealing your child's identity. It came back showing that Todd has money in this bank."

"Hmm." Jack skimmed over the statement. "This is weird. I didn't think banks could do that without all kinds of personal information. That's a lot of dough. Do you think Ray did it?"

"That's what Todd said. I guess it's possible, but not real likely. Unless he's just feeling tremendously guilty, which I doubt."

She told Jack about her other theory, about the possibility that her father had socked away the cash for Todd.

Jack shook his head slowly. “We’ll go into the bank. They must have something about the person depositing the money.”

Maddie nodded thoughtfully. Taking the report back, she glanced over it also. This time, she noticed something she had missed before. “This says the bank is in San Francisco.” She put the paper back in her purse.

“Great. We can have a little getaway and visit the bank in person.”

“There’s something else. Unrelated, but also weird. A painting was delivered, to me, on Friday. In all the excitement I forgot to show it to you when you picked me up.” She described the gift to Jack, who now seemed more concerned. And while he didn’t say it, she knew he suspected Ray of meddling with her life.

They stopped for groceries before picking up Todd. Even shopping together was a new joy. He liked sourdough; she wanted whole wheat. She reached for margarine, he insisted on butter. She was out of decaf; he threw French Market Roast into the basket.

“I suppose you buy those wimpy short paper towels too,” he complained, a package of *Brawny* in his hands. Maddie began to giggle hysterically, causing stares from passing shoppers. She was laughing too hard to reply, so she simply plucked the towels from his hand and tossed them into the cart.

“Thank you!” he said, rolling his eyes.

They continued to banter as they unloaded the groceries at the check stand. The cashier smiled at Maddie, shaking her head comically. “Haven’t seen you in a while.

You're brave to be shopping with your husband," she teased, looking from Maddie to Jack. "I'm used to seeing you with your son."

Maddie returned the smile, noting the slight lift to Jack's eyebrows. "Brave doesn't begin to describe it."

Todd helped them unload the grocery bags. "All right!" he exclaimed, pulling a box of Frosted Flakes from the bag. "Thanks, Mom."

"Thank 'Junk Food Jack'," she answered with a wink.

"Hey," Jack began in defense. "I let you buy all that broccoli and crap."

"You said you loved broccoli!"

"I do." Jack came up behind her at the counter, wrapping his arms around her and kissing her neck. Maddie quickly glanced at Todd, who was already pouring out a bowl of cereal. Jack sensed her apprehension; she was worried about how her son would react. Ray, it seemed, had never shown affection in front of the boy, or anyone else for that matter. "All in time," he whispered, and Maddie turned a grateful smile his way.

They made dinner and ate it together, the three of them, despite Todd's sugar-coated appetizer. Before they knew it, it was late, a Sunday night, and Jack put on his jacket. In the family room he found Todd watching TV.

"I gotta go, sport. But I wanted to talk to you about something."

Todd sat up from his slouched position on the couch, attentive.

"When's that beach trip you were talking about?"

"It's in a couple of weeks. At the end of school. Why?"

"Thought maybe you wouldn't mind taking me along."

"You mean it?"

"Of course. I haven't been camping in a while, and I'd love to get out there. I even have all the gear, stashed away in my loft. What do you say?"

"I say great, Jack. Great!"

"Good." Jack sat down on the corner of the couch. "Todd, I know it hasn't been easy for you around here, what with Ray and all. Your mom shared with me all that about your real dad, too."

Todd's eyes looked solemnly back at him.

"I just want you to know, I really care about your mom *and* you, and if there's anything I can ever do for you, you just let me know, okay? Is that a deal?"

"Yup."

Unable to help himself, Jack stood and leaned down to kiss the top of Todd's head. "See ya later, son." He pretended not to see the single tear that slid silently down Todd's cheek.

At the front door, Jack said his good-byes to Maddie.

"Now, I don't like this at all."

Maddie bit her lip and shrugged.

"This is going to get old, real fast." Jack held her by the shoulders. Still she didn't respond, and he sighed. "Okay." He kissed her then, hoping it would be enough and knowing it wouldn't be.

"We'll figure something out," she murmured, her own voice husky with desire. "I promise."

"You bet we will."

And so the week ended and another began, with everything the same and yet so very different. During a meeting with Paul, Maddie was promoted, and Della was to be her personal assistant. The two women went to lunch to celebrate.

"Maddie, you are absolutely glowing, more, if that's

possible. Was it a nuclear power plant or just Jack?"

"Jack, Jack, Jack! Oh Della, he is positively the most wonderful man in the world."

"Oh darn. That dashes my plans..."

Maddie smiled at her friend, who was thirty-five and never married. Tall, slender and copper-haired, Della would be a catch. Maddie did not understand why she remained alone.

"So obviously things progressed," Della baited, clearly hoping Maddie would tell all.

"You could say that."

"So what happens next? You moving in with him or he with you? Or are you going to try the "I-get-the-bottom-drawer-in-your-dresser" technique? Could be the, "maybe-the-kids-won't-notice-your-underwear-on-our-clothesline" challenge." Della had obviously experienced both.

"Funny you should mention that," Maddie said, pensive. "I haven't figured out what to say to Todd."

"How old is your son, Maddie?"

"He just turned twelve."

Della made a sound of dismissal and waved her hand. "What are you worried about? He already knows you and Jack got it on in Tahoe. What's the diff?"

At Della's frank words, Maddie looked at her in alarm. "You think so?"

"You don't know your son very well, do you?"

"Of course I do. We're the best of friends."

"You're also his mother. He's your baby. Listen Maddie, at twelve, believe me, *he knows*. Does he like Jack?"

"He loves Jack. But how can you say…"

"I know. I…I have a son of my own. He's twelve also, and he's pretty savvy. But besides that, you should always remember what they say, what's good for the mother is good for the child."

Maddie looked closely at Della. "You have a son?"

"Yeah. Lives with his dad, in Austin. He's a sweet boy. Maybe next time he's out here, I'll bring him in and he can meet Todd."

Maddie had a lot of questions, but felt she didn't know Della well enough to ask them. If Della wanted Maddie to know, she'd tell her.

"I say, grab that man before he cools off. Drive that damned truck of yours over to his place, load up his shit and him, and bring him home, girl." Della tapped her finger in demand, her southern drawl creeping into her speech.

Maddie laughed at Della's directive, nodding. Maybe she should do just that.

The following Saturday morning the three of them set out for San Francisco. June came in with a moderate heat wave, and the Golden Gate shone bright tangerine in the pre-summer sun. It was a first for Todd, whose camera clicked repeatedly from the back seat.

Jack pointed out the sights as he drove.

"I spent a couple of weeks up here once with Carol," he told Maddie. "That's Alcatraz, Todd. Over there."

"Who's Carol?" Todd wanted to know.

"My ex-wife," Jack called back to him.

"I think everyone in the world is divorced from somebody," Todd commented, his camera clicking. Jack and Maddie exchanged glances.

The bank was downtown, and after almost a half hour of seeking a place to park, the threesome walked through the doors of City Trust Bank. Jack charmed the first teller into interrupting the bank manager, who seated them in the New

Accounts department and went in search of the department manager.

Maddie was jittery. She wasn't certain what they would find out or even if she really wanted to know. There was an ominous feeling, a feeling that it could somehow threaten her new life, and she didn't like it.

New Accounts Manager Fred Nalley sat down before them.

"I understand you have a question about your account?"

"Yes," Maddie began, retrieving the identity report from her purse. "This account was set up in my son's name by an unknown benefactor. It has become very important for us to identify the person who was so generous."

The manager looked over the page.

"The gentlemen who initiated this account had all the necessary information to open the account. It was not necessary for us to verify his identification. He deposited cash, and since he had the boy's taxpayer I.D., well…that's really all I can tell you."

"Do you remember the guy?" Jack asked.

"Somewhat, yes."

Hastily Maddie fished her wallet from her purse and unsnapped the section containing photos. Sliding one from its sleeve, she held it out to Fred Nalley. "Is this the man?"

Nalley looked at the photo of Ray Tyler. "No. Definitely not. This man was older, much heavier. I do remember him saying it was for the son of a widowed friend, if that helps."

Maddie looked at Jack in disappointment. While relieved it wasn't Ray, she now had a worse problem. A total stranger had her son's social security number and address.

Jack broke the silence on the way to lunch.

"If you like seafood, I know a great place down here at Pier 39. After that, we'll walk over to Ghirardelli Square and load up on chocolate."

"I'm with you, Jack," Todd answered happily. Maddie could tell he was tiring of the mystery and wary of what it all meant.

After lunch they played tourist and visited the shops along the pier, bought their chocolate and watched street puppeteers dance their marionettes. Harbor seals entertained them, and walruses, a bane to the boat owners, basked lazily on the dock. Tired, they at last trekked back to Jack's car and he drove to their hotel.

It was a two-room suite. Maddie was the only one who seemed nervous about their sleeping arrangements while Jack and Todd tossed a souvenir 49ers football between them. A kitchenette adjoined the suite, complete with a microwave, a small refrigerator and a table. Jack ordered a pizza and sat down to watch television.

From the small kitchen, Maddie watched the two of them sitting on the couch together, thinking nothing looked more natural. Of course, the show of choice was a hockey game; the San Jose Sharks were winning. For sake of argument, Jack supported the losing New York Rangers, and he and Todd got into a playful punching match with each penalty or goal.

It had been a very long day for Maddie, fraught with questions and frustrations. Leaning across Jack, she kissed Todd goodnight on the forehead.

"Sleep well, darling," she whispered.

Pausing over Jack, she kissed his forehead as well.

"I'll be there in a minute," he said. "The game's almost over."

Ah! He said it. Right in front of Todd. Maddie blushed but neither of them seemed to notice.

She was still awake when Jack slid into bed beside her thirty minutes later.

"I tucked your baby boy into bed. He's fine."

She was on him immediately, holding him tightly in her arms. He chuckled softly, nuzzling her ear.

"This is really hard for you, isn't it?" he asked.

"I guess so. I don't know. I don't know anything anymore except that I love you and I don't ever want to sleep away from you again."

Maddie fell asleep almost immediately in Jack's arms.

"Do you mind if I open this up?" Jack asked as he felt along the back edges of the framed painting Maddie had received. On his knees on the family room floor, he picked carefully at the wire staples holding the cardboard backing in place.

"Go ahead," Maddie replied, opening a soft drink and sitting on the couch. The drive home had been uneventful, and upon arriving at Maddie's, Jack had asked to see the painting.

Slipping the backing off, they could see the back of the canvas where it had been fastened to the frame. And in the corner was a gold-foil label.

"Wait, wait, wait… here, it says, *Perrault Studios*, Paris, France."

"Let me see," Maddie said, joining him. "Wow. Paris."

"But you said it was mailed in Switzerland."

"Yeah, but you know, it's right next door…"

"Right next door, huh?" Jack grinned at her. He put the frame back together and wiped his hands on his trousers, then sat on the couch. "Well. What do you want to do? Forget about it? Worry about it? What."

"I don't know." She sat down also, and he put his arm around her affectionately.

"My guess is that our old buddy Ray is messing with you. But if you want, we can go exploring again."

"Right. You just going to drive me to Paris?"

"I will if you want me to." His tone was now serious.

Maddie thought quietly for a moment. She'd wanted to return to France since she and Thomas had left there fourteen year before. "Okay," she said with a smile, playing along with his offer. "Will you take me to the top of the Eiffel Tower?"

"Of course, my love."

He went home then, saying he needed to feed his fish. And when she challenged him, saying he didn't have any fish, he asked her how she knew.

At work the following morning, she was more than happy to hear his voice on the phone. She had decided not to worry about the painting, to instead concentrate on how she was going to get Jack to move in with her. His question threw her.

"You do have a passport, don't you?"

"Why, yes. Yes, I got it when Ray and I…oh, never mind. I do have one. Why?"

"Dust it off, baby, we're going to France."

"*What?*"

"You heard me. I got a deal on the tickets, if we're willing to go standby. We'll leave in ten days. I have to finish this model I'm working on."

Confusion flooded her mind. *France?*

"It'll only be for a couple of days."

"I'll have to find somewhere for Todd to stay."

"You will. It'll be fun."

Maddie hung up the phone, dazed. Della looked up from where she was re-shelving law books on the wall.

"What's up?"

"Jack's taking me to Paris."

"And you're not jumping up and down? What's wrong with you, girl?"

"I hate to keep pawning Todd off on his friends. I have no relatives. Jack has mentioned a couple of times that Todd could stay with his folks out in Palm Springs, but…they're total strangers and his dad is, well, a tough old bird by Jack's own admission, and…I just feel guilty."

"Well Maddie, I don't know how you'd feel about it, but…" Della's voice lowered. "I'll take him anytime you want. Kevin—that's my son I told you about—he's coming to stay with me for a couple of weeks. I'd love it if he had someone to play with. I'm so worried he'll get bored while he's here, and I so want him to enjoy himself."

"Della, that's a wonderful idea. Thanks, thanks so much!"

"Hey, I'm happy to do it. Just make sure you bring me one of those miniature Eiffel Towers."

Jack was pleased with his decision to take Maddie to France. It bothered him, the painting arriving so mysteriously, the savings account in Todd's name and the personal information its benefactor held. Sure, they could try to get in touch with Ray. And Ray would deny having anything to do with the mystery. No, taking Maddie to Europe would be a lot more fun, and Jack wanted to get the answers to Maddie's questions, to get past the whole ordeal and move ahead to better things: their future together.

He also wanted something else. There was still a tiny

ache in his heart, something unfinished and gnawing away at him. There was another life in this world for which he was responsible, a life just beginning with a future so uncertain and unknown. Jack's desire to hold his own young son close was increasing with his love for Maddie and Todd.

The fact that he was traveling abroad gave him reason to call. He wanted Kelly to know where he would be, should any emergency arise in his absence. Her voice was cool and unaffected on the phone.

"I'd like to see him before I go," Jack asserted. From his balcony he watched children on the street below playing Saturday morning tag.

"It's not convenient. I'm taking him to the beach with me today for a photo shoot."

"Leave him with me."

Kelly uttered a mirthless laugh. "What would you do with him for seven hours? You can't even change his diaper."

Jack started to challenge her comment, and thought better of it. Closing his eyes, he ventured on. "I'll pick him up in thirty minutes. Just pack his little duds and his diapers. You can call me when you get back."

"Jack…"

"We'll do just fine. Half hour." He hung up, holding tightly onto the leash that controlled his anger.

Kelly Mathis was not a bad mother. Looking around her small living room, Jack could find no visible fault with Duncan's environment. His toys were appropriate and safe; his robust demeanor and advanced development told the story of a happy, well-adjusted babyhood. Standing at the coffee table, treating Jack to a droolly, toothy grin, Duncan waved his small hand up and down while he proudly held onto the table with his other.

"You do have a car seat, right?" Kelly was asking while packing cans of formula into Duncan's bag.

"Uh, no. I'll need yours."

Kelly sighed in disgust. "Well go get it then. Car's in the garage." She tossed him a set of keys and Jack set his jaw.

Car seat and diaper bag in place, Kelly passed Duncan over to his father at the curb. Jack hugged him briefly before settling him into the seat and carefully locking the straps around his small body. Kelly leaned into the backseat afterward, testing the straps and kissing Duncan's baby fine hair.

"You have fun with Daddy," she murmured. "Mommy will be back real soon."

Grudgingly, Jack thanked Kelly and got behind the wheel. With one eye constantly checking his rear-view mirror, Jack drove across town, his thoughts jumbled and disturbing. He should have remembered about the seat. He didn't ask for the stroller, already too angry with himself and with Kelly for her lack of compassion. It was with a small sense of surprise that he now realized he was driving down Maddie's street and not his own. Her truck was in the driveway.

"We have a little friend today," he said to her astonished face at the door. Speechless, she held open the screen door for him and watched with amusement as he carried Duncan inside.

As if she did it every day, Maddie took the baby from him and Duncan wrapped his small arm around her shoulder for support.

"I was wondering if you might be able to do some shopping with me," Jack asked, his smile both innocent and calculating. "Dunc here needs a few pieces of equipment."

"I'd love to."

They spent the day together, buying a car seat, stroller and highchair, playing with Duncan and enjoying each other's company. Subtly, Maddie taught Jack how to feed and diaper his small son, imparting the motherly advice he was missing by not living with Kelly and Duncan.

"He still uses a bottle all the time?" she asked, watching Duncan play with the nipple on the bottle Jack had put before him.

"I guess, hell, I don't know."

Maddie left them and returned a few minutes later with a small cup with a sipper-style lid.

"This was Todd's. I kept it all these years—don't ask me why—but I'll just bet…" She carefully poured the formula into the cup and secured the lid, then placed the sipper into Duncan's mouth and tilted the cup.

A look of surprised delight came across the baby's face, causing the formula to run from his mouth and down his chin. Jack grabbed a washcloth but Maddie shook her head, again tilting the cup. Again Duncan smiled and drooled. Jack held his tongue, watching the process with fascination. By the fifth try, Duncan was gulping the formula, choking some, his tiny hand holding one handle on the cup while Maddie held the other.

"Amazing." Jack shook his head.

"He's ready. At least for daytime."

"What would I do without you?" Jack caressed her cheek with the back of his finger.

He deposited Duncan with his mother at 6:00 p.m. Kelly seemed disappointed, somehow, that Duncan appeared so happy and cared for, arriving in his new car seat unscathed. After exchanging tender good-byes with his son, Jack flashed Kelly a rueful smile.

"By the way, I put a couple of new sipper cups in the bag. He's ready, at least for daytime." He touched his forehead thoughtfully before adding, "And Kel, I wouldn't bother with those plans to go to New York, unless you're planning to go by yourself."

With Kelly's mouth gaping, Jack took his leave.

Eleven

"This seemed so much easier in my old Dodge Charger," Jack groaned, adjusting his position a third time. The back seat in the Acura just wasn't quite wide enough to accommodate them, and Maddie snickered.

"I'll bet. Oh, what I wouldn't have given for a ride in that car." Maddie sighed as Jack kissed her neck repeatedly.

She felt his fingers sliding up her back beneath her sweater, and a shiver went through her. A sweet, sensual shiver that she imagined continued through him as well.

"You could have ridden in it any time, my love. All you had to do was ask."

"Jack, the windows are so steamy I can't see the movie!"

"You're not supposed to be watching the movie, Maddie." He chuckled then, his lips against her ear. "You *never* made out in a car?"

"No," she gasped, breathless. "Never. I wasn't allowed in boys' cars."

"Ooh, baby," he teased.

"Ooh baby," she echoed, now kissing his chest, her fever building.

He lifted her chin, peering at her in the darkness.

"You've got a hickey on your neck the size of Texas."

"Oh my God, Jack, no!" she said in horror. She could imagine the looks she'd get at work, let alone trying to hide it from Todd.

"It's your own fault, lady."

Maddie rushed her fingers into his hair and shook them, giving him an even more disheveled look while he again struggled to find comfort in his cramped position.

"I have to make up for my lack of talent on the rink," she said softly.

"You have all the talent I'll ever need," he said, holding his hand against her cheek. "Ever."

Soon he started the engine, turned on the defroster and the windows began to clear. The movie was largely ignored, the old, crackling speaker turned down low. Jack held Maddie comfortably against his chest, settled back against the pillows he'd stuffed into the corner of the backseat.

"I like this. Good idea, driving out here. This must be the last drive-in theater in Southern California."

"Well, it's only fair, since we didn't get to do it back then."

"Do you remember your senior prom?" Maddie asked.

"Sure. I danced with Melinda Middleton, Jackie Bates, Kathleen Anderson…they all asked *me*, mind you."

"Do you remember the punch girl?" Maddie asked through pouting lips. "I had to join ASB just to be able to volunteer."

"Do you know how many times I started up there for punch, only to turn chicken and go the other way?"

"Sure."

"No, it's true. And the last time, I figured I'd better go through with it, because you'd seen me coming." Jack chuckled. "Man, I was some kind of wuss."

"And that's when there was that awful blast outside…"

"And I followed the others out there to see what it was."

"That creep Joey Hicks had flushed a firecracker or something." Maddie had hated Joey ever since.

"An M-80 in the boys' head. I remember it well." Jack sighed comically. "When I got back, you were gone."

"Your loss."

"Yup. My loss."

His expression turned serious. "Tell me about Thomas. About your life with him." His hands were back under her sweater, his arms wrapped securely around her midriff. It was a delicious intimacy, and Maddie savored his touch.

"Well, we lived in the canyon. He had this funky house built into the hillside, with a little greenhouse attached onto the back. He loved butterflies, studied them, chased them, but never caught them. He always said their lives were short enough. He thought it was hilarious that I was afraid of grasshoppers and crickets, and he was always trying to get me to appreciate the way the crickets sang at night.

"In the evenings he would translate French novels to me. I was into pottery then, I'd be up to my armpits in clay, I had a wheel then, too. Sometimes I'd be on the floor hooking a rug. I guess I was a bit of a late-blooming flower child."

She took a moment to catch some more memories before speaking, and to stroke Jack's cheek with her hand. "I was *Madeleine* back then, you know. That's what Thomas called me. He was born and raised in central France. He grew orchids, rare ones and easy ones, and other exotic plants in the greenhouse. Sometimes we'd join other professors and their wives. Sometimes they'd assume I was Thomas' daughter. He was so…mature, you know?"

"I can understand that," Jack said quietly.

"Tom had a real daughter, still living in France. She

was only seven years younger than me. She addressed her letters to "Papa," so I started calling him that as a joke. So we were 'Madeleine and Papa'."

"What happened to his first wife?"

"His *only* wife," Maddie corrected. "He never told me. I assumed she was dead. I never asked more. He had his little...privacies. He traveled a lot, too. For his job."

"As a tutor?"

"No, he wasn't a tutor anymore. That's why we came back to the U.S. It was for a job. He was a correspondent or something. He translated things, and met with people."

Jack found it odd that Maddie knew so little about her lover's past. How his wife had died seemed like such an important question. But she didn't even know what he did for a living?

"He was a real gentleman, Jack. You would have liked him. He was kind, and strong, and protective."

Like a father, Jack thought with irony. He wondered when Thomas had first taken Maddie to his bed. Was she sixteen? Seventeen? He couldn't ask. No, Jack was not certain he would have liked Thomas LaForge all that much. But he kept his thoughts to himself.

He also wondered at the wisdom in taking her to France. What would they find? He was putting his chips on Ray Tyler. And he could not, would not, let Ray hurt Maddie again. Never.

Maddie was kissing his neck again, and Jack closed his eyes. Melodrama was not his forté, but his love for her exaggerated his fears. She was his now, and he would gladly put himself in harm's way for her if necessary.

Kevin Spaulding was taller and ganglier than Todd, but

he held in his hand the ultimate communication device of today's adolescent: a controller for the latest and greatest video game deck. Todd was immediately impressed and pulled his own travel-controller from his backpack. The two boys were soon running down the hall toward Della's guest room, temporarily set up for Kevin's stay.

"I don't know how to thank you, Della. And please tell Paul again…"

"Yeah, yeah, like you already told him ten times, thanks for the time off, I know. You kids just have fun over there. *Parlez vous fran-sez*, and all that stuff."

Jack squeezed Della's shoulder.

"We do appreciate this."

Della smiled coyly at Jack.

"My pleasure. You just bring her back in one piece. I can't handle her work too long by myself."

"Isn't it obvious?" Jack responded to Maddie's questions on the way out of the building where Della lived. "Kevin was the product of an affair. My guess is, the dad was and is a married man."

"Awfully judgmental, aren't we?" Maddie sniffed, getting into the car.

"Just sounds about right to me. His father somehow won custody, or maybe your friend didn't feel she could raise a child alone. Some women feel that way, right?" He stuck the key in the ignition and turned to look at her, his eyes solemn.

Maddie caught his meaning. She herself had panicked and made a bad decision in marrying Ray. But, she reminded herself, it was important at the time. She would have done anything to give Todd a chance at a happy life.

"He was lucky. The dad, I mean. I, on the other hand,

have little chance of gaining custody of my son."

"What do you mean?"

"Paul says, basically, that because I'm not married, and I don't have a swing set in my yard or a live-in Mary Poppins, Kelly will probably get to raise Duncan. With whomever she pleases. I'll be lucky to get every other weekend and a Christmas here and there. It sucks."

Maddie nodded. It was, indeed, a sad situation, and one she intended to think more about. When they returned.

The jet took off ten minutes late, but soon they began the long flight that would have one stop over in New York before crossing the Atlantic. Jack's moodiness rendered him quiet. The day had started on an awkward note, with Maddie asking if he would go with her to the cemetery to visit Thomas' grave before they left. Although it was the last thing he wanted to do, he complied and trudged up the grassy knoll at Eternal Rest.

She brought flowers, and Jack stood back while she knelt and placed the small bouquet. When she rose, her eyes were moist and she hugged Jack, who returned her embrace tenderly.

"It's an awful thing to drown in the ocean, Jack."

"I know, baby. I know. Come on. We should get going."

He remembered staring at the headstone. Thomas LaForge would have been forty-six years old by now. And his charisma, whatever it was that drew Maddie to him, still reached beyond the grave to tug at her heart.

Jack ordered a Bloody Mary and pushed his seat back. He wished this mess were over. He wished Ray would take a fall and that Thomas' ghost would find someone else to haunt.

They would put the whole affair to rest, in France,

come home and make some important decisions. He was not yet bold enough to buy the ring, but Jack had already proposed to her a hundred times in his mind. He just needed to be sure she was ready. Timing could be everything.

He stole a peek at her. She looked troubled, staring out the window at the nothingness that engulfed the jet, thinking about what? Thomas? Ray? Todd? He hoped it was not himself—not with that sadness in her eyes. Jack finished his drink and closed his eyes for a nap. A long trip lay ahead.

"Paris is for lovers," the poster in the airport declared. The sights of the infamous city seemed to cheer Maddie, and despite their fatigue they both excitedly identified the landmarks they had expected to see. It took Jack a while to get used to the small, inexpensive rental car with the bad clutch, but soon they were maneuvering around the city in search of their hotel. But not before stopping at the Tower.

"It's incredible," Maddie said, taking a deep breath of cool air. "It seems so powerful, and being able to see so far gives you such a sense of greatness. If only it were true."

"On the contrary," Jack answered with a sigh. "In the face of this greatness, I feel pretty small and insignificant."

Maddie slipped her hands inside Jack's windbreaker and around his waist, pressing her cheek against his chest. "You are anything but."

They rented an upstairs flat in Montmartre, a small, eclectic district of Paris known in English as the Mountain of the Martyr, or "Martyr's Hill". Once there, they each showered and dressed for an evening out. The proprietor who lived on the first floor provided suggestions and soon they were dining in an intimate cafe two blocks away. Jack was relieved that he did not have to hunt out an eatery after dark in the rental car.

Amid candlelight and violin music, they stared into each other's eyes for what seemed like hours, not speaking, each reluctant to voice their fears and expectations. They sampled wonderful French cuisine and laughed at Jack's comical observations. Jack ordered the finest local wine available and they toasted the future.

They took their time walking back to the hotel, looking into the tiny shops and markets. The June night was splendid and for a time they could forget whatever problems they had, real or imagined.

The rooms in the flat weren't large but were blessed with plenty of charm. The double bed squeaked, the toilet ran, but neither noticed. A bowl of fruit graced the table in the living room along with the last of the wine they'd brought from the bistro. The flat offered no television or phone, but there was a tiny, narrow kitchenette. The exceptionally thick walls boasted windows and doors, arched in an historic architecture. The windows swung out over the cobblestone street below. Jack opened them all before turning out the light.

"Picasso's 'hood," he murmured. "Hard to imagine all that went on here."

Once in bed, Jack turned to Maddie and touched her on the nose. "Hey."

"Hey," she repeated, grasping his finger and kissing it.

"Still love me?" he asked, tracing around her mouth with his finger.

"Still love you."

"Well, I guess tomorrow's a big day. You realize we may find out absolutely nothing."

"I know."

"And we may find out something unpleasant."

"I know."

"Okay. As long as you're prepared."

"Make love to me, Jack."

It was all he needed to hear.

Morning dawned early. There were no "black out" draperies in this room, only aging curtains that partially covered the window. They showered, dressed and went downstairs and out to the street.

The proprietor was serving breakfast and invited them in. There were omelets and crepes, a variety of delicious pastries and meats. Jack headed for the coffee, delighting in its strong flavor. Maddie, also partaking of the coffee, ate little.

Their host provided them with a rudimentary map and telephone directory, and with Maddie's halting French they were able to obtain directions to the art studio. With the rental car balking and jerking, they were on their way.

Henri Perrault was on the sidewalk sweeping up glass from a broken storefront window. His expression clearly warned that he was not a man to be trifled with today.

Maddie was jittery. She looked to Jack for help.

"Monsieur Perrault?"

"*Oui*."

"Uh, we need your help, *si vous plait*?" Jack said, now wishing he'd taken French in addition to Spanish.

"*Oui?*" The shopkeeper stopped sweeping and waved his arm toward the shop.

"Can I help you?" a young girl wanted to know. *She must be about Todd's age,* Jack thought.

"You speak English?" Jack asked.

"Yes. My father does not. I can help you."

"We're trying to find out something about one of your

customers. He had a painting framed in this shop, probably very recently."

"What was the painting of? Perhaps my father will remember." She looked at Maddie with curiosity.

"Here is a photo." Maddie took a moment to retrieve the photo on her cell and handed the phone to the girl. The girl put it before her father who looked at Maddie and squinted.

"*Oui*."

"He remembers."

"Good! I have a picture of the man that may have ordered the work. Can he look at it for me?" Maddie hastened to get her wallet out of her purse once again. Jack nervously glanced around the shop wondering if some evil force lurked behind the black curtain leading to the rear.

Maddie thrust the photo of Ray before the surly Frenchman, who shook his head in exasperation.

"*Non. Non.*" Not his customer.

Maddie's hands shook as she tried to push the photo back into the sleeve. "Might as well throw this away. No reason to keep it," she muttered. In her haste and confusion, the wallet slipped from her hands to the floor.

"*Zut Alors!*" the man cried, squatting to pick the wallet from the piles of glass fragments. Some of her other photos had fallen out and he retrieved these as well. Suddenly he became animated, spewing a stream of French and looking from Maddie to his daughter and back. He pointed excitedly at a photo of a man, saying, "*Trés jeune, oui, c'est l'homme.*"

"My father says this is the man, only when younger. He's right, I remember him. A very nice man."

In horror, Maddie and Jack looked at the photo in the shopkeeper's hand. It was the snapshot signed, "Love, Papa."

Jack helped Maddie into a seat at the sidewalk cafe next door. Pale and trembling, she stared vacantly at the street for some time. Jack grasped her hand in his, alternately squeezing and kissing it in an effort to bring her back to him. The distance was widening and he didn't know what to do.

He ordered them sandwiches and beers, but Maddie took only the beer.

"Maddie, honey, I can't imagine how this must feel to you. There must be some mistake. We'll get to the bottom of it, I promise. Okay? Please baby, please talk to me."

Maddie turned a bleak smile his way. "Yeah. It's okay. I'm okay." She coughed a little, and then straightened up in her chair. "I never mentioned that they didn't find his body, did I?"

Jack's face now paled. "That grave we went to yesterday is empty?"

"Yes."

Jack now took a long draught of beer. The fear that had been gnawing away at him suddenly grew larger. The fear he couldn't quite identify, the unreasonable doubt he'd suffered, now had a name. Thomas LaForge. Not Ray Tyler.

Maddie spoke again. "We need to find Monique."

"And who is Monique?"

"Tom's daughter. If we find her, we'll find the truth."

A few doors away, they saw a placard displaying an ascending jet, so they packed up their sandwiches and began to walk. Jack wanted desperately to flee, to turn Maddie by the shoulders and drive her straight to the airport. But the wheels were turning and there was no stopping now.

The travel agent was friendly and spoke perfect English.

"All I remember is that they lived near the Loire River," Maddie explained.

"Oh, my dear, the Loire River Valley is very large and contains hundreds of towns, villages, burgs. You'll need more than that to find your friend." She referred to a large map behind her on the wall. "You may look in my directory if you wish."

Together they hunched over the phone book, but could find no Monique LaForge listed.

"Surely she's married by now," Maddie said sadly.

"Perhaps you can find out the name of the town where your friend was born?" the agent asked. "Did your friend apply for any credit, schooling, driver's license, marriage license, anything like that in America? If so, there should be records, and they may be more easily attained than those here," she suggested.

Jack watched Maddie closely as her expression went from one of quiet introspection to sudden enlightenment.

"School records…Southwestern. Paul."

Moments later, Jack used his credit card to call the United States, using the innkeeper's phone. Once the call was connected, he handed the phone to Maddie.

"Paul, I need your help. It's really, really important." Maddie described the situation briefly and asked Paul to find out. She knew he could do it. Paul hesitated and then agreed to try.

"I'll call you back just as soon as I have something."

Maddie sat on a small settee, her arms folded across her chest. If Tom was alive, why did he fake his own death? Why would he hurt her so? She began to bite her cuticles.

Jack sat beside her and pulled her hand away from her mouth. "Don't."

She turned on him then, unable to keep the irritation from her face, and briskly pulled her hand away. Jack held his hands up and stood, backing away without a word.

Angry at herself, Maddie got up and approached him, tentatively reaching out to embrace him. “I’m sorry, Jack,” she murmured. He hugged her back, rocking her much like the night in her kitchen so long ago.

“Shhh. It’s okay.”

The minutes on the clock ticked by. Jack checked his watch again and again, and when the phone finally rang it was he who got to it first.

“Yeah, Paul. It’s Jack. Thank you. I’ll write it down.” Jack scribbled on a note pad.

“Jack? How is Maddie doing? She sounded pretty upset,” Paul wanted to know.

“Well, it’s to be expected, don’t you think?”

Jack heard Paul sigh.

“She’s not going to find the answer she is looking for,” Paul said softly. “Stay close, Jack. This isn’t going to be easy.”

“You got that right. Thanks again, Paul.” Jack felt ill. This scenario was worse than any he could have imagined himself. The dead ex-boyfriend rises to steal away the woman of his dreams. He paced the room, alternately looking at Maddie and the street through the small window.

Neither of them slept well. There would be no lovemaking tonight, no playful frolic or tender whispers in the dark. Maddie drifted far away and Jack could not reach her. He eventually gave up trying. It angered him that he had no control, no way to get through, no way to direct the outcome of the inevitable. Around midnight he got out of bed and dressed.

“Where are you going?” she asked in the darkness.

"I need to take a walk."

"Don't go."

"I have to. I'll be okay. You get some sleep."

He was gone for two hours, walking through the sleeping neighborhood, breathing deeply of the cool air, sometimes shaking his head in an effort to clear it. *Montmartre. God, I don't want to be one.* He relived the memories of his six months with Maddie.

Maddie, sitting on the park bench just looking at the sky, an open book in her lap. *She didn't even see me,* he thought, *until Duncan jettisoned his bootie onto the sidewalk. But I saw her.*

Maddie, sitting across from him in the coffee shop, coyly reminding him about his missing graduation, her stalking him in vain. He never told her that he'd really only broken one arm on the ice. The other his father had broken later that night.

What would she say about that now?

She had cheered for him at the rink.

Then there was Maddie looking out across the marina, telling him her terrible secrets, and letting him kiss her that night on the driveway. Instinctively, he looked up; there was that nasty old moon again, hanging right over his head.

And Maddie, tearing open his shirt in the back seat of his car, holding him tightly and making everything about sex into everything about love.

She was sleeping when he returned, probably out of sheer exhaustion, he thought. Careful not to wake her, he slipped quietly into bed and wrapped one arm around her. Soon it would be morning and their fate would be known.

Twelve

It was a two to three hour drive from Paris to Rochecorbon, a small village near Tours in the Loire River Valley. Once they got out on the highway, the car ran better and it was a smooth ride.

They spoke little. Jack lamented about what a wonderful drive it could be, for they passed castle after castle along the way. Enormous, majestic castles, many with moats and drawbridges, steeples and turrets. And wineries abounded. Some of the finest wines in the world were created here. Jack shook his head.

He looked over at Maddie from time to time, always finding her staring into the distance. She seemed blind to the castles and the vineyards, unaffected by the fine weather or the breathtaking sight of Loire whenever it wandered into view.

Finally she returned his gaze, reaching over to squeeze his hand. "This must be hard for you, too," she said quietly.

"Naw. It's nothing for me. Shit like this always happens, boy meets girl, boy falls in love, girl's dead ex materializes, sends her gifts…"

"Jack, that's not fair." She looked away again.

"Maybe not."

The sign ahead finally displayed the words they were

watching for: "Rochecorbon, 2 km." Compared to the sprawling, sparkling city they had left behind, Rochecorbon was a mere whistle stop. Jack got out of the car and sauntered up to the window of a petrol station, where a woman eyed him suspiciously.

"*Oui* Madame, we are looking for *la maison d'LaForge*."

The woman pointed to a dirt road at the end of the street, motioning for them to take the road to the right. Toward the river.

"*Merci*, Madame."

"*Trés bien*," she muttered, closing the window.

Jack drove the car to the end of the street and pulled over. He turned to Maddie. "Well dear heart, this is it. I don't know any more than you do about what we will find. But before we take this road, I need you to know something.

"When I offered to bring you here, my intention was to put you straight about Ray. I was convinced it was he who had sent you the money and the photo. I guess I was wrong. Had I known this involved Thomas, I wouldn't have come. I would never have even opened the frame."

Jack paused to collect his thoughts, looking ahead through the windshield. In the far distance he could see a large farmhouse near the river. "But here we are. I don't have those choices now."

"Jack, don't worry so," she said softly.

"How can I not worry, Maddie? How can I not…" He sighed heavily. "I guess I just want you to know that I love you, and regardless of what happens here, I will still love you."

It wasn't what he really wanted to say, but it would have to do. He couldn't very well tell her he wanted to take her home and forget about all this mystery crap. He couldn't tell her that Thomas was really dead, let's just leave him that way. He couldn't tell her how he'd planned to propose to her last night, until things had changed.

And amid all the turmoil and confusion Jack felt, all Maddie could do was reach out and squeeze his hand once more. Jack put the car in gear.

The farmhouse was large and inviting, with a wraparound covered porch complete with rocking chairs and tables. Living vines of startling color climbed to the second floor. The view from the porch was of the river, of course, and Maddie tried to link it to a story Thomas may have told her. She could think of none.

A woman stood on the porch, watching them approach. Drying her hands on her apron, she looked from their car to two little girls, running around in the yard, one chasing the other and laughing. "Nicole! Jeanne!" She waved them in and they went running toward the house, the woman following them inside.

Maddie got out of the car, her knees feeling wobbly. A hot breeze seemed to come out of nowhere, fluttering her blue cotton dress. Self-consciously she smoothed it down around her legs, and from the corner of her eye she caught Jack watching her. They walked together to the door and Jack knocked.

The same woman they'd seen earlier on the porch answered. She ignored Jack's polite but broken French and stared openly at Maddie before speaking. "Madeleine? Is it you?"

Maddie stared back. The woman appeared to be about thirty, with large, dark brown eyes and thick brown hair. The eyes were familiar, and Jack saw it too. They were Todd's eyes; more, they were Thomas' eyes.

"Monique," Maddie said at last.

"*Oui!* Please, come in. Oh, my. Does Papa know you are in France?"

Those words confirmed everything. Maddie grasped the doorjamb to steady herself. "No. I don't believe he does."

They were shown to a small parlor just inside the door where they sat together on a flowered couch. Maddie looked around the room. Signs of Thomas were everywhere. Butterflies, flowers, books. A small brick fireplace stood at the end of the room, framed photographs littered its mantel. From where she sat, Maddie could distinguish several photos of herself, and school pictures of Todd. A small snapshot, yellowed with age, of Maddie and Thomas.

Maddie glanced at Jack, who also studied the photos. She wondered, fleetingly, what he was thinking when at last he tore his eyes away from the mantel and closed them briefly.

Monique brought in a tray bearing a pitcher of iced tea, and Jack accepted a tall glass. "This nightmare is becoming more bizarre by the moment," he murmured.

"The little girls, are they yours?" Maddie asked.

"*Oui*. Nicole et Jeanne. How do you say? They are born together."

"Twins." Maddie smiled at Monique, still in awe of her beauty and likeness to her own son at home. "Is he here? Thomas?"

"No. He is away. He stays...well, there will be time to talk about that." Monique poured two more glasses of tea.

"How about we talk about that now?" Jack said tersely. "Where is he, and why hasn't he contacted Maddie to let her know he was alive all these years?"

Monique colored. "I cannot answer for my father. He has his reasons."

"Reasons so important that he would let the woman

who loved him suffer? So important that he would ignore the son he fathered and obviously knows all about?"

"Jack, please. It's not Monique's fault."

Jack huffed out a breath. "I'm sorry. But maybe you can get your father on the phone or something? Tell him we're here and we'd like some answers."

"There is no phone at the lighthouse and no wireless service. If you want to talk to him, you will have to drive there."

"And where is 'there'?" Jack asked.

"An island off Brittany. In the northwest of France."

"Oh, he's shacked up in a lighthouse on the Brittany coast? Must be nice."

Maddie sighed. "Isn't this difficult enough? Do you think you can just calm down a little?" She turned to Monique. "I'm sorry. We're still reeling. This lighthouse, is it easily accessible?"

Monique nodded. "If you know where it is, it's an easy walk from the highway."

"But there's no way to let him know we are coming."

"Non." Monique tossed back her hair. "But he will be glad to see you."

"I doubt that," Jack muttered. "Not when he hears what I have to say."

Once back on the highway, Jack was quiet.

"You are more upset than I am. I'm sure there is a good reason."

"I'm—I'm just blown away by all this, Mad. I don't know what to think."

"Then don't think. Let's just find him and then we'll get to the bottom of it."

"I can't believe you are so calm. He's been dead to you,

for how long?"

Maddie licked her lips. "I'm not calm, all right? I'm a wreck. Inside, I am churning. Can you imagine? Yeah, he's been dead for twelve years. He was, I thought, my lifetime partner. My baby's father. And then, poof! He was gone, without a word. I imagined, daily, how horrible it must have been for him to drown in that cold water. I grieved. So badly." Her voice broke with the last words of her diatribe. "But the fact remains, he's alive, he obviously wanted to reach out to us, and I can't just ignore that. As much as part of me wants to, I just can't get on the jet and go home now. Right? Do you get that, Jack?"

Jack didn't take his eyes off the road ahead, but eventually reached over and took her hand. "I do. I do get it. I'm just scared out of my wits."

The Phare de l'Ile Lighthouse was located on the property of a large coastal estate. Decommissioned in the 1960's, the lighthouse was now a private residence and no longer used as an aid to navigation, although its light was reportedly still operational. Jack parked the car at the end of the driveway, the closest access point to the lighthouse. They got out and went through an unlocked gate, per Monique's instructions.

The walk was about a quarter of a mile, on a dirt path through low, overgrown vegetation. The tip of the tall, rectangular tower eventually peeked over the top of the trees, and Maddie felt her stomach cinch. She hadn't lied when she told Jack she wasn't calm, and with each step, her anxiety increased. What would they say? What would Thomas say? How would he look? And most importantly, how would she feel? She'd loved him obsessively.

The exterior of the lighthouse was in disrepair. The tower adjoined a small house that probably consisted of four rooms. The door and trim needed sanding and painting. Jack paused only a moment and then rapped on the splintering wood. After several moments, he turned to Maddie. "Maybe he's not here after all."

Maddie shook her head. "After that five hour drive, he'd better be here." She knocked again, so hard the wood surface abraded her knuckles. Finally, the door opened, and Maddie drew in a quick breath.

He was thinner, tanner, and crow's feet had grown from the corners of his eyes. He leaned upon a cane.

"Sorry, I was in the tower. I saw you coming; I should have started down sooner. Bonjour."

Unable to speak, Maddie stared. Jack swallowed, then pushed back his hair. "You must be Thomas."

"Yes. Please, come inside."

Jack stepped aside so that Maddie could precede him into the small house. Maddie couldn't take her eyes off of the man who should be a ghost.

"Madeleine, it's...it's so good to see you."

Maddie finally found her voice. "And you. I'm...I don't know what to say."

Thomas's ebony eyes fixed upon hers, until at last he turned away. "So my dear, at last you know the truth." He looked down for a moment, then back to her face. "I cannot ask your forgiveness, only that you listen to my story with the compassion I know you still have."

Maddie was transfixed. Thomas was not only still alive, but he could walk, and talk, and was still charismatic. His hair was very long, only slightly streaked with silver, and pulled back into a queue. His eyes were keen, delving, and they looked at Maddie with longing and regret. And except for the cane, his body looked strong and healthy for a man who should have been long dead from the disease that wracked his body when she saw him last.

"Please, relax in my home. It's small, but adequate. And you are Jacques."

"I'm sorry, of course. This is my friend Jack. He was good enough to bring me all the way over here to…to find out what was going on," Maddie explained. Jack flinched, and Maddie glanced at him briefly.

Thomas nodded. "Yes, I know. Let us sit down. *Ma chérie*, may we have some *citronade, si vous plait?*"

In her shock at seeing Thomas alive, Maddie knew she had missed something, something very important. Looking back to the doorway, she stared in awe at the blonde woman standing there.

"Hi Maddie. Yes, it's me."

"Elise? What the hell?"

Thomas spoke again. "I can explain. For now, let it suffice to say that Elise is Monique's sister-in-law. She is family."

"But I thought you were with Ray!"

"I just arrived here yesterday," Elise said.

"*That's Elise*?" Jack blurted out.

Maddie nodded, looking just as confused as Jack sounded. "Thomas, I think you have a lot of explaining to do. But I'm not sure I'm up to it. This is all, really, quite a shock," Maddie said softly. Instinctively, Jack wrapped his arm around her shoulders, a move not lost on Thomas, who pulled up the ottoman. He sat near them.

"I know, *ma petite*. You did not deserve this kind of surprise. I should have contacted you a long, long time ago. Alas, I am not the man you thought I was."

"That's for sure," Jack mumbled. "She thought you were a *dead* man."

"I was wasting away, Maddie, or so I thought. I

suffered long and hard over my decision. Yes, I steered directly into the storm that day. I knew squalls had been reported. I was depressed, I was despondent. I could not go on."

"Do—go on," Maddie said levelly.

"The news I had gotten that day was not that I would die; on the contrary, I would live, but I would live a crippled, gnarled life, with no control over my faculties. I could not do that to you, my dear. It would not be fair. Your love was so great, your faith in me so strong; I knew you would insist on staying with me and waiting on me when I could no longer help myself. And that, I felt, was a fate worse for you than my death. So I tried to die."

Maddie gave a little sigh. She remembered the day like it was yesterday. He'd called to say he was finished at the doctor, and he felt good. He was just going down to secure the boat, as a storm was coming in.

"*Tried* to die?" Jack found and squeezed Maddie's hand. "Surely you're not falling for this line of bull…"

"When I washed up on a beach the next morning, I hoped no one had seen me. My plan was formed. I left for France a few days later, with the help of a friend.

"It is a long and tedious story, but the doctors in my country provided treatment I had not been offered in the U.S. My condition began to improve after about a year. After another year I was nearly cured. Except for this," he said, gesturing to his left hip.

"You could have let me know." Maddie's voice was small but firm.

"I considered it, many times. Especially when I found out you'd borne us a son."

"So you do know about Todd."

The atmosphere in the room had gone from tense to nearly unbearable. Jack began to wish he were anywhere but where he was sitting. Thomas's manner grated on him big time.

"Todd is a wonderful boy. I am extremely proud. I wish…"

"You wish what?" Jack could not hold his temper a minute more. "That you could have been there to cut the cord? That you hadn't missed his first step, his first cold, his first black eye? That you could be there to take him to hockey games and teach him how to be with a woman?"

"Jack!" Maddie was visibly astounded by his angry words.

"*Non*, Madeleine. Jacques is correct. I have been remiss." Thomas shook his head.

"You're damned right you've been remiss. You've been *more* than remiss. I can't believe we are even sitting here listening to this sob story, Maddie. Aren't you just the tiniest bit disappointed in this aging Casanova?"

"Please, Jack! Don't." The tears now bounded down her cheeks and she pressed her fingers to her lips.

Thomas held up his hands in a gesture meant to calm. "I am sorry. Now I have also caused discord between you and your lover. I am a foolish man."

"Ah. I have graduated to lover! That's an improvement," Jack said in disgust. There was a terrible, hideous silence in the room, the only sound coming from Maddie's attempt to stifle her sobs. Jack stood up. "Why did you do it? Why now? You could have just stayed dead. What did you hope to gain with your mysterious packages, your 'gifts,' the insidious clues to your identity? You hurt her once, now you're hurting her again. How could you just screw with their lives like that?" Jack was almost too enraged to talk. He turned his glare upon Elise.

"And you! How can you even show your face? You seduced her husband! You people think this is fun? This is sick, you're *all* sick."

Maddie looked up at him in anguish, and Jack held his own hands up in a hopeless gesture. Then, he squatted before her, ignoring the others in the room silently stirring their drinks and pretending the outburst hadn't occurred.

"Maddie…" He took her hand in his, rubbing it with his other. "I'm sorry I brought you here, but I won't apologize for the way I feel. I need to get some air. You take your time; talk to your…" he cleared his throat and continued, "… him. I'll be outside."

Maddie touched his cheek gently before he stood and walked to the door.

"And by the way, the name is *Jack*, not Jacques. I am American, not French." With his last biting comment still stinging his tongue, Jack left the house.

"Well. *He's* got a hot head," Elise commented, taking the pitcher to the kitchen to refill and leaving Thomas and Maddie alone. Thomas shrugged.

"What a miserable mess I have made, eh Madeleine? The best laid plans, as they say." Thomas stood and walked slowly to the window where Jack had stood before. In the sill stood a framed wedding photograph of Maddie and Ray—a smaller version of the same one she had at home. "I was so excited to get this one, when you married Raymond. He looked like such a nice young man. *Mais oui!* What a scoundrel he turned out to be, eh? If only I had known."

"You've had someone spying on me all these years."

"I still loved you. I needed to know that you were safe; I was living with such guilt, my darling. I was crushed when

I found out you were carrying our child. And me, playing possum, thousands of miles away. No help to you. I enlisted the help of a friend to watch over you for me. You haven't figured it out by now?"

Maddie shook her head, dabbing at her eyes.

"No one I know or care about would deceive me so." She thought for a moment. Did she still even know anyone she knew back then? Both her parents dead. She had not kept in contact with any of their mutual friends, most of them being older than she.

"How did you find me, Madeleine? We lived in Tours, but surely you did not remember Rochecorbon yourself?"

Maddie paled. *Paul*. Paul had been the spy. Paul had taken some of those photos himself! Paul had quietly passed on the information, the details of her personal life, never letting on that he had anything more than a remote knowledge of Thomas LaForge. It was even Paul who set up the account for Todd, the "son of a widowed friend."

Dear Paul. Desperate to defend Paul to herself, she reasoned that Paul thought it in her best interest. He was good to her, a wonderful boss and friend. He'd even told Thomas about Jack, she realized. And when she'd needed him, he was always there.

"For the record, I did not send you the painting. That was Elise's meddling. I did not know about it until after she had put it in the post. I don't know what she was thinking, except that she was angry with me for disapproving of her behavior with Ray."

"What *about* Elise? How did she get involved with Ray?"

Thomas' face again bore a tragic mask.

"When I began to hear stories of Ray's... indiscretions, I was incensed. I wanted to kill him. How could he?"

Thomas stopped, his fists tightened as if he thought of using them against Ray. “Elise was here. She was leaving for the States, and I asked her to check on you. To see if it was really true, that Ray was fooling around with others. She was more than happy to get involved and prove what a scoundrel he really is. I did not realize how far it would go.”

Maddie’s throat tightened. So it was worse than she’d thought. Elise was not even the first.

“I see,” she said weakly.

“I’m sorry. You did not know.”

“It’s water under the bridge, now.”

“I suppose so.” Thomas walked to sit beside her in Jack’s place. Putting his cane aside, he slowly put his arm around her. “Madeleine. I want you to know something. For whatever it is worth, probably nothing…” He paused to draw a deep breath. “What I did was very, very wrong. I caused you enormous pain, and I would do anything to undo that damage. In spite of it all, I love you every bit as much today as I did that day so long ago, you are still my girl, my love, and my heart’s desire. Your happiness means everything to me.”

“What are you suggesting, Thomas? What is it you want from me?” Maddie’s eyes were dark with pain and disillusionment.

“Only that you give me a chance to earn your forgiveness. Let me convince you that my intentions were good even if my methods were the wrong ones.” He paused. “If you were to stay, just a little while, perhaps we could mend fences. We have so much catching up to do.”

Maddie looked away from him. Through the sheer curtains she could see Jack, walking slowly along the path, his hands thrust deep into his pockets. He was looking up at the sky, and she wondered, was he seeking answers also?

Turning back to Thomas, she tried to weigh his words. Did he want her back? Was he offering to return to the living? She wasn't sure she understood his intentions, but could not formulate the questions she needed to ask. Not yet.

"You think it over. We have plenty of room, and it would be nice to get to know you again, *chérie*."

"I do need to think about all this." She took another tissue and wiped her cheeks. "May I use the bathroom?"

"*Certainement*. It is there. Off the hall."

Maddie left the room and went to wash her face and hands. She began to finger comb her hair, then paused, thinking she heard voices. The vent above the mirror must adjoin the kitchen, she thought.

"He wants to marry her," Elise was saying.

"Of course he does."

"They say it's because he has a baby son. The mother won't give him up without a fight, and the courts say he can't have the kid without first having a wife."

"It is too bad. She would be happier with me."

"Perhaps. But Jack's got her thinking he's in love with her. He is determined to get the baby." Elise sounded certain.

"How do you come by this news?" Papa's tone was skeptical.

"Some here, some there, some is just damned obvious."

Maddie could not believe her ears. Could it possibly be true? Jack was using her to get Duncan away from Kelly?

Her heart began to pound. She pressed her palms to her face and stared into the mirror. She didn't even recognize herself anymore. Her life had twisted and turned and twisted some more. Oh, if only they hadn't come! If only she'd never met Jack, if only she'd never married Ray. If only Thomas hadn't gotten sick. She felt suddenly dizzy and sick all at once. Quickly she opened the toilet lid and expelled what little food was left in her stomach.

Again she washed her faced and again she vomited. Would this nightmare ever go away?

Finally, more pale than ever, she left the bathroom and went into the pleasant little kitchen. Elise stood alone by an open window and quickly threw a burning cigarette into the sink.

"Maddie, you look like hell. Are you okay, honey?"

"I'm fine. It's just a little warm, and I didn't eat much breakfast. It's a lot of excitement, you know?" She leaned against the doorway for support. "Elise, I didn't know you were French."

"I'm not. My real name, my "American" name, is Elizabeth. My brother Tony married Thomas's daughter Monique."

"Oh. I see."

"Well, except that he died," Elise added.

"Oh, I'm so sorry, Elise. And Monique must be devastated, with those two beautiful daughters."

"So, are you and Jack shacked up?"

At the sound of Jack's name Maddie felt sick again. "No. I live with my son." Could what she overheard Elise say be true? Where had she gotten the information? Same place, she thought sourly, that Thomas had gleaned so much about her. Quickly she changed the subject.

"How was my husband when you left him?"

"Ray? He was hanging by a thread, so to speak," she said happily. "I pretty much told him where he could stick his piton."

Maddie smiled bleakly. It wasn't really very funny.

"You want something to eat? I'm afraid you're gonna faint right here."

"Where is Thomas?"

"He said he left his daybook in the tower. There's some ham and cheese if you want a sandwich. Maybe a little glass of wine?"

"No, really." Maddie sat down and averted her eyes. "I'm having trouble digesting all this."

"I have a suggestion. Stay with us for just a day or two. Let Thomas make his apologies. Get to know him again. Perhaps things will seem…more clear then."

As if reading Maddie's mind, Elise continued. "Send your lover home, for now. He's pissed off and upset. He can't do any good here now. Then, something will shake out. If it's right to be with him, you'll know. If it's right to be with your ex, you'll feel it."

Maddie was surprised at how simple Elise made it sound. Was it? How could she tell Jack to go home? How could she stay in this house with the man who had left her alone for nearly thirteen years?

These and other questions pummeled her tired brain. Wearily she rubbed her forehead. No, there was nothing simple about her situation.

"Hey, cowboy, wait up!" Elise called, trying to catch up with Jack as he strolled along the beach. The sun had already set, and the sea had darkened.

"I beg your pardon?"

"Cowboy. That's what some of the locals call American men."

Jack didn't respond.

"He wants her back, you know."

"What?" Jack stopped walking and turned toward Elise.

"Tom. He wants Maddie back. He's been trying to talk her into staying."

Jack frowned and resumed his walk. He didn't appreciate this bad-mannered stranger talking about Maddie. She talked as if it was of no consequence that the best thing that had ever happened to him might not be happening to him at all. He kicked at a rock, sending it sailing into the surf.

"Look, Elise. I'd kind of like to be alone."

"Sure Jack. Just thought I'd warn you. And if she stays, hey. Maybe I can use her ticket home." With that she turned back toward the house, pausing only to launch one more barb. "And by the way, it was no big deal with Ray. It wasn't like I was the first." It was all Jack could do not to flip her off behind her back. *Meddling bitch.*

Thirteen

Jack tired of walking and sat down beneath a tree near the edge of the lighthouse property. Instead of dispelling his anger, it had only grown, fueled by the irony of the beauty around him. He loved the island, loved the sight of the water. The warm air, the squawking of birds, the sound of the surf. It was all too lovely to be wasted.

He sensed Maddie's approach before he turned to look. He thought about getting up but decided against it. He was just too mad.

Maddie sat awkwardly on the ground beside him. Tentatively she touched his shoulder, but he didn't respond, his frown fixed on the dark blue horizon.

"I need to ask you something, Jack," she said softly.

"Shoot."

Maddie grimaced, but continued. "Is it true that you, that you…want to marry me?"

Jack turned to look into her face. She now had his attention, and he tilted his head slightly to one side. "What brought this up?"

"Is it true? I need to know."

Jack looked back to the water. "Seems to me you already have two men in your life. Can't imagine you needing a third just yet."

"Oh damn it Jack, just answer me! Are you...*were* you planning to ask me?"

"Yes. Of course. And you had to have already known that."

Maddie wet her lips and took a deep breath. "Is it also true that you planned to sue for custody of Duncan, after we were married? I mean, if we married?"

Jack frowned. "Yes. And you knew that, too. C'mon Maddie, what is this all about?"

Maddie turned her eyes away, and then posed a third question. "Did Paul tell you that the only way you could get Duncan was to get married?" Her voice was so small the breeze threatened to carry it away.

Jack fell silent. It took him a minute before enlightenment and rage filled his face simultaneously. He jumped to his feet, startling Maddie.

"Just what the HELL are those people telling you in there? Do you honestly think I would marry you just to get my son? Is that what you think? Because if you do, you're just as crazy as those loons in there! I am...I am stunned, Maddie. Stunned that you would think that about me. That you would even entertain the idea."

Jack began to pace wildly back and forth. Maddie stood and backed away. "Jack, stop. Please. Talk to me. Jack, please!"

Jack approached her, grasping her wrists tightly and pulling her close to him. His voice was low and pained. "Don't you see what they're doing? They are screwing with us. For some reason, they don't want us to be together. That little slut Elise was out here, telling me you might stay here. That I might be going home without you. Is that true?"

"I-I don't know. I need to think. I'm confused, Jack. I'm scared. Nothing is right, everything is upside down."

Jack softened his grip. So it was true. She was actually considering it. Staying here with Thomas. His worst fears, fears that seemed so irrational last night, now rose up before him like a black wave he couldn't escape.

"I need time, Jack. I don't know what is happening, who to believe…yes! I'm spinning out! You waited for me before, can you do it again? Will you? I need to be sure I'm doing the right thing."

He dropped his arms to his sides, defeated. When he spoke, his voice was weak and sullen. "How can you just walk away, Maddie? After everything we've said, everything we've been to each other. Don't…do this; don't ask me to wait. You want that broken down guy in there, that lying, selfish, deceitful fraud? Can he make you feel the way I do, the way we do when we're together? Can you ever trust him, can you give him your trust and your honesty, the way you gave it to me?" He made no effort to wipe the tears from his eyes. "He left you, Maddie. Left you alone and pregnant."

"He didn't know I was pregnant."

"Even after he did know, he knew everything about you, knew you were in trouble, did he come back? Did he call? No! He left you to suffer." He was yelling again, his arms raised in disgust.

"Jack, we were together five years! I can't just turn my back after so long… He was my first love."

Jack stopped pacing and looked at her.

"I thought I was your first love."

"You might have been…if we had ever gotten the chance to get close. But you were gone. He was there; he helped me get through it. He loved me so…so completely."

"You were a child. A child looking for a father's love," he murmured, not certain she should hear his last words. Taking a few slow steps toward her, he embraced her firmly, burying his face in her neck. The ever-increasing wind blew her hair across both their faces. "You know I love you," he whispered, his voice choking, "but I can't deal with this. I will get on that jet tomorrow, alone, and I will go back to a boy who is waiting for me to take him on a camping trip. *He* is the boy I would call my son. *He* is."

"Jack, I am so sorry…" she began, her own tears mingling with his.

"Of course I will wait for you." His promise was firm but barely audible. *I have no choice. I'm in too deep. My entire soul is invested in you.*

He pulled away then, and walked the short distance to the car. He would not look toward the lighthouse again. He opened the trunk and lifted out Maddie's suitcases, setting them near the beginning of the walkway to the porch. Then he got behind the wheel.

"You're not leaving now*?"* Maddie called, running to the driver's side door.

"That, I am. You need to stay and finish this. I won't marry a woman who will always wonder, and you will always wonder if you leave with me now." Jack gave her a level look, the tears gone. Calm at least on the surface, he reached up to caress her cheek as she leaned close to the car. "I have a plane to catch."

"But it's dark. Where will you stay tonight? Stay here, Jack. Please."

"There's something you should know about me. I am not a religious man, in the traditional sense. I tend to see my God in the people and things around me, and that's where I place my trust and faith. I'm leaving that faith with you now, Maddie. And if you're not strong enough to handle it, I hope He is there behind you to help.

"Don't make me wait too long. You have to decide

what you want. You know what I have to offer you. But if you're looking for another father figure, I'm not your guy." Jack paused, breaking his gaze decisively and looking toward the rising tide. Finally turning back to Maddie, he touched her cheek with one more, brief, tender caress, then turned the car around and headed back down the dirt road.

Maddie grasped the handles on her rolling suitcases and dragged them slowly back toward the house. Consumed with despair, she paused upon reaching the porch and glanced skyward, absently tangling her fingers amid the windblown locks of hair around her face. She wished the heavens would deliver an answer to her dilemma. Jack's words bounced around inside her head, heaping more torture upon her already aching soul.

Father figure. Was that all Thomas had been to her? The thought had no sooner crossed her mind than a movement in the upstairs tower window caught her eye. In an instant, the subject of her question had moved away, dropping the lace curtain back into the windowsill.

Inside the house, Elise met her at the kitchen door, a fresh cigarette lodged between her fingers.

"Is there somewhere I can lie down?" Maddie asked.

"Of course. We have a room back here."

Maddie fell into a deep sleep. The nights before had been rough, today even worse. She was emotionally spent and physically burned out. She woke on the bed with a cool, damp cloth across her forehead. She opened her eyes to find Monique hovering.

"Bonjour! You are awake. How do you feel?"

"I don't know. I'm numb from the brain down."

"Brain?" Monique was puzzled.

"*Tete*. No feeling," Maddie demonstrated by knocking on the side of her head and Monique laughed.

"Is it morning? What are you doing here?"

"Papa asked me to come down and look after you. Are you feeling better?" She stopped beside the bed and turned the cloth over, taking a moment to peer deeply into Maddie's eyes with a smile. "Your Jacques, he is *trés bien, oui*?"

"*Trés bien*? He is good, yes." Maddie returned a weak smile. "Very good."

Monique nodded. "He is, ah, hand-some."

"That too," Maddie agreed, now beginning to feel dizzy again.

"Papa, he wants to talk to you. I tell him, non; she is resting."

"Thank you, Monique. I did need to rest. I am still exhausted."

"J'ai fait cuire le petit déjeuner. I hope you will eat with us."

"My French is pretty rusty, but I think I heard the word 'breakfast' in there?" Maddie was actually hungry. She liked Monique, liked her easy manner, her simple way of looking at things. How sad to be a widow so young. Young and alone. Like me, she thought with irony. *Like me*.

"Where is everyone else?" Maddie asked, seeing only the young girls seated at the table.

"Elise has gone. Papa gave her a ride."

"Gone? Where?"

"She has returned to America," Monique answered, placing a large platter of croissants and tartines on the table. "Papa took her to the train in Brest this morning."

"Really. Wow." Maddie's stomach churned. "I wonder where she's going?"

"She has a house in Los Angeles. She has a...a...job in a café serving."

"Good. She needs to keep busy." *And away from Jack.*

The meal was delicious and filling. Monique prepared a perfect espresso, one Jack would have appreciated, Maddie thought ruefully. She helped Monique clean up afterward and then walked outside to sit on the porch.

Visions of her days in Tours with Thomas wafted slowly into her mind. Sunshiny, happy days, hanging out with his scholarly French friends, dining lavishly, drinking lots of local wine. *I was so young. So naïve.*

"We did live high on the hog," Maddie murmured. There was always plenty of money, more so, of course, when Thomas returned from a business trip. In retrospect, now that she knew more of life and survival, the money seemed out of proportion with what Thomas professed to do to earn it.

Once, while attending a play, Thomas was approached by a stranger with an anguished face. Maddie recalled that Thomas had taken the man outside to talk, and had returned to the theater alone. When asked about the strange occurrence, Thomas had merely shrugged it off. "A friend of Lilly's. He didn't know she had died. He thought, perhaps, that I was behaving inappropriately."

Maddie sighed and got up to take a walk around the grounds. The midday sun was exquisitely bright, the breeze warm and embracing. She walked inland, away from the water, exploring the uneven island terrain. An old fort stood about a kilometer away, and Maddie took time to walk around the architectural wonder. The fort, she'd heard, had once been owned by a famous French actress.

Sitting atop a low stone pillar, Maddie pondered her situation. Jack would soon be boarding the jet for home. Thomas was likely back from the nearby town where he dropped off Elise. At home, she hoped Todd was enjoying his time with Della and her son. And here she sat, trying to sort her jumbled thoughts.

After another hour or so, she meandered back to the lighthouse. She circled the small building after noticing a fenced area in the rear. The gate was unlocked, so she ventured into the roughly tended garden. Half of the area boasted growing vegetables and fruits, the other half, uncultivated but pleasantly filled with wildflowers surrounding a stone bench. Drawn to this charming setting, Maddie again sat down. She was not yet prepared to face Thomas.

Her eyes perused the garden while she imagined her former partner on his knees with a claw and trowel. His touches were here, to be sure. Trellises were carefully tended, supporting climbing tomatoes and beans. Only the area directly behind the bench seemed completely raw. Except for a small, concrete square. Her interest piqued, Maddie swung her legs over the bench so that she could face the other direction and get a better look at the square. Vines and foliage had grown over part of it, so she crept closer and knelt. A quick intake of air marked her realization that the concrete marker was a headstone.

"Lillian Aileen LaForge. *Elle était une femme bien-aimée et la mère.*" Horrified to discover that Thomas' wife was buried beneath her feet, Maddie took a step back and stumbled against the bench. She understood enough to pick out the words for "wife" and "mother."

"Are you enjoying my garden?"

Thomas' voice behind her gave Maddie another start. She turned to face him. "It's very nice," she managed. "So Elise left?"

"Yes. But do not be concerned. She is not on the same

flight as Jack."

"As if that matters. If she wants to go after Jack, she won't need to be on that jet."

"She won't. Trust me."

"Trust you? Ha!" Maddie walked around to the front of the bench and sat down. "Bad choice of words."

"Figure of speech," Thomas muttered.

Her thoughts naturally turned to Jack. She wondered what he was thinking. She hurt him badly, she knew, and she regretted every word. But the doubts remained, just below the surface.

"If only we could rewind," she said softly, running her fingers along the rough edge of the bench. "If only we could take back our mistakes and re-record the right things…"

"I've wished that a hundred times. A thousand times. But that wish never comes true." Thomas joined her on the bench. "How many times have we wondered what lies on the road we did not take? Questioned the decisions that have brought us to today?"

Maddie nodded in silent agreement. Indeed, she thought. *Like me wishing earlier that I hadn't come here.*

"I scared away your young man, didn't I?" Thomas said without looking at her. "I am sorry, ma petite. He is right to be angry with me."

"He was out of line, Papa. He doesn't usually act like that. I didn't understand it."

Thomas seemed warmed by her use of her old nickname for him. He patted her hand.

"I do. And you will probably have to get used to it, if you stay with him, that is. But you will only see it when you are digging too close to the heart." He chuckled softly. "We backed him against the wall, did we not? Don't worry, my darling. He will not go away. Not if you don't want him to."

Maddie turned her eyes on Thomas. His words puzzled her. "You sound like you want me to stay with Jack. Yesterday, you were asking me to stay with you. Am I wrong?"

Thomas sighed and took her hand. "You have grown into a wonderful, strong, capable woman. Yet you still have the beauty of the young girl who sat in the front row of my class. Who would not want you to stay? Ah, I told you. I am a foolish man. But not so foolish that I would let you marry another imbecile like Raymond."

"What do you mean?" Surely he did not think Jack anything like Ray.

"Madeleine. You think I was rambling on my sentiments yesterday for nothing. It is true that my fondest wish is that you forgive me. But it is my ultimate wish that you are happy. Do you know what I saw out my window last evening?"

"No, what?"

"Ah. I saw a man filled with passion. A man so consumed with love that his every breath is for his woman; I saw this man strong enough to show his tears, brave enough to walk away, trusting that she will follow.

"You think I want to get in the way of that kind of passion?" He chuckled again. "Jacques, excuse me darling, *Jack*, he could be the husband you have always wanted. Always needed. He is already yours, forever."

Despite her pain, Maddie smiled to herself. So Papa had seen all that.

"You know what else I saw?"

"No Papa. What else?"

"I saw myself. Twenty some years ago. Right there." He paused to point to the same area she had stood earlier with Jack. "My fingers were bleeding. Something to do with that tree, over there, and my own untamed temper. She was leaving me, or so she said, for the city lights of Paris. I was in such a rage it scared her and she started to cry. I felt like an ass. Indeed, I was one."

Thomas examined the back of his knuckles as if he could still see the blood. "She did not leave me. She said," and at his memories Thomas began to laugh, a hearty laugh erupting from deep within, "she said I was a danger to myself, that I couldn't be trusted, that she had to stay to keep me alive. Ha!"

Maddie smiled. He was talking about Lilly, his first wife, something he never did while they were together. She tried to envision the two of them, screaming and arguing under the shadow of the tower, the sea smugly roaring in its infinite knowledge of their smallness, their brief moment in the sun.

Thomas's laughter died away. "Imagine that, she staying to keep *me* alive. But I could not do the same for her." A melancholy pallor spread across Thomas' rugged face. He suddenly looked much older to Maddie's watchful eyes. So Lilly *was* dead.

"How did it happen, Papa?"

"A bus accident, in Tours. Lilly was on her bicycle."

"When?" Maddie's curiosity overrode her reluctance to make fresh his painful memories.

"We had only been together about two years. She was almost twenty. Monique was an infant."

"I'm so sorry, Thomas."

He waved his arm in dismissal. "There are those who say I was trying to replace Lilly when I brought you home."

"Were you?"

"Perhaps."

Maddie digested this newest lightning bolt into her past.

A replacement for his dead wife. Should she be angry? How many shortcomings could he ask her to forgive?

Despite her uneventful day, she was suddenly very tired. The answers would have to wait.

Jack tossed his keys onto the counter. He'd slept fitfully on the flight and was in no better, perhaps a worse, mood than when he left France. Rubbing his eyes, he hit the button on the answering machine then picked up his mail. The only thing of interest was a letter from Paul Adams. Probably just his bill.

The messages were all job-related. Grabbing a note pad from next to the phone, he jotted down a couple of phone numbers.

The teakettle was already on the stove, and he considered some coffee. Instead, he opted for whiskey. Filling a highball glass with ice, he poured out a healthy slug of Irish rye and plopped himself onto the couch.

Jack was more than just angry. He was disappointed in himself for the anger. All the years he had spent working on controlling his temper, trying to rid himself of the only noticeable trait he shared with his father, and he'd blown it all away so easily yesterday.

He was also disappointed in himself for not foreseeing the inevitable; genuinely pissed off at himself for leaving Maddie in France with a man he considered lower than pond scum. He took a gulp of the whiskey, swallowing fast and feeling the fiery liquid burn its way to his stomach. Why did he come back? Was it really because of Todd?

No, he had to admit. He left because he was afraid. Afraid to watch the all-powerful Thomas work his magic on his love. His soul mate. His would-be bride.

Jack closed his eyes. Maddie was sitting beside him on

the coast of France, reaching out to touch his shoulder. He squeezed his eyes tighter in pain. She was scared, she said. She had been told something nasty. Something about his wrong intentions. And how had he responded?

"Jack, Jack… You're such a friggin' ass."

He took another swallow, this time not noticing the burn quite so much. His eyes were open now, but he was still with Maddie at the lighthouse.

"I'm confused," she'd told him, begging his understanding and help. He might as well have slapped her face. So who was more scared? Who turned tail and ran away?

"I left her there with a lecherous, crippled charlatan."

Jack downed the last of his drink and went back to the bar to refill it.

"Thanks, Dad," he said loudly, holding the bottle up to inspect the label. "Thanks for the booze, the broken arm and my wonderful self-control."

"You never have any decent Irish liquor in this place," his dad was saying, coming in from the balcony to voice his complaint.

Jack spun around, but saw only his own reflection in the sliding glass door. Slowly he brought the glass to his lips and drank down almost half of the drink.

The airline food was not fit for a dog, he decided, and had avoided all but a few pretzels on the way home. The rye in his stomach boiled and stewed. And not being accustomed to hard liquor, Jack was soon staggering to his bedroom.

Placing his again empty glass on the nightstand, he pulled his shirttails from his pants and began working the buttons. He hadn't quite finished when he fell backwards onto the bed; like a crazy carousel, his room whirled around him.

"Oh, Maddie…" he whispered miserably. "I'm sorry,

baby. I'm so sorry. I hope you know. I hope."

Fourteen

The sunlight splashed in through the window, its healing rays bathing Maddie with a warm radiance. Still half asleep, she slid her fingers across the too-soft mattress in search of her sometimes bed partner but found only blankets and sheets. She opened her eyes.

The room was cheery and feminine. The wallpaper was old and flowery, the bed quilt thick and hand embroidered. A washbasin stood against one wall, with a silver comb and brush beside the bowl and an antique mirror set above it on the wall. In her turmoil, Maddie had not acknowledged the room's beauty on the previous morning.

She was in no hurry to get out of bed. Slowly, the painful events of the previous days seeped into her head, one by one giving her pause and remorse. She sighed, remembering Jack's parting words and Papa's confessions of the afternoon before. Letting her mind wander, she recalled the Thomas she'd once known. So even-tempered, so full of gentle grace, Thomas never spoke an unkind word or raised his voice to her. Always generous, always patient, always true. He was a slave to her happiness.

Deep within her, Maddie understood why Thomas disappeared. He would no longer be able to walk with her through the gardens. No more would they take the "Jeune

Fille" out of the marina or picnic at the beach. His beloved little Renault would have been sold, replaced by a wheelchair. It would have been she bringing him breakfast in bed rather than he carting in the fabulous French cuisine he brought her each Saturday morning.

But now, all was changed.

Thomas had recovered. Maddie relived, for a moment, the enormity of the emotion that washed over her at the sight of him when he opened the lighthouse door. A living ghost; her cherished partner, protector, and paramour, returned to her in the flesh after so many, many years. Not only was he her first lover, he was the father of her only child. The father so badly needed and wished for.

Ah, Thomas could teach Todd so many things. Certainly Maddie had tried to bring what wisdom she could to her son, always feeling she was just short of what Todd really needed. The possibility that Todd could finally meet his father intrigued her. But did Thomas want to meet his son?

Later that morning, she watched Papa play with his granddaughters in the garden, their shrill giggles carried by the wind. Panting, he joined her on the small porch.

"You would feel at home here, Madeleine," Thomas said, catching his breath. "You and Todd. The living is slow, and easy. The school is right down the road. But non! Todd would be already going to the middle school, as you call it! Ah, I have missed so much." His eyes reflected regret as they followed the young girls playing tag. "It is no problem to send for Todd. I have the funds."

"Of course you do, Papa, and I'm thankful for your offer, but…"

Thomas held up his hand. "I understand. I do not wish to rush you."

Now, Maddie puzzled over Papa's offer. Just last night, he described Jack as her perfect mate. But was he?

Leaving Thomas behind, she walked down to the beach and spied a couple nearby, picnicking on the sand. On their flowered blanket sat a little boy, probably a year old, drinking from a heavy ceramic mug. Maddie was immediately reminded of Duncan and the day she taught him to drink from a cup.

Oh, Duncan. Is it true? Would your daddy be willing to marry just to have the chance to raise you?

Jack's words floated around her head like gnats. "*...because I'm not married and I don't have a swing set in my yard or a live-in Mary Poppins... I'll be lucky to get every other weekend and a Christmas here and there.*"

She sat down at the water's edge.

"Oh, Jack. I thought you loved me. I thought I loved you." She pressed her forehead against her raised knees and cried. Maybe she was just confused. That whole scene before he left, the anger, the tears...how could he not be sincere?

With her heart filled with stones, she slowly walked back toward the lighthouse.

His face inches from the bathroom mirror, Jack peered closely at his eyes. They were red, of course.

God! I never looked this bad on my worst day in college!

His shirt reeked of whiskey; he quickly balled it up and tossed it into the hamper.

A long shower repaired some of the damage, but he knew it would take more than hot water to fix what was broken. He was determined, however, and no longer afraid. Because without Maddie, not a hell of a lot mattered.

In the other room, he squatted down to examine the

elaborate model that was in progress. He had about fifteen more hours on it, he figured. But not today. Today he was going to pick up Todd, and he was going to have to put on hold this and any designs he harbored for winning Maddie back. If she *could* be won, he reminded himself drearily.

Downing a quick cup of coffee, he pulled a card from his wallet and picked up the phone. Della answered the phone laughing, infecting Jack with a smile.

"Del? Jack. You got my boy?"

"Sure do. He's been anxious for your call. They've been up for *hours*," she complained.

"Burning up the video games, no doubt."

"Yup. Still at it. Come over anytime. We'll be here."

In the car, Jack wondered how he would explain Maddie's absence. He'd think of something. He didn't think she would want Todd to know the truth, not just yet.

Todd's gear was neatly stacked beside the door.

"As you can see, he's ready to go," Della pointed out. "We loved having him."

"We loved you having him," Jack responded, grasping the straps on Todd's duffel bag.

"Maddie at home?" she asked casually.

"Ah, no. She's not."

Todd raced in from the back bedroom. "Jack! You're here!"

"Hey sport, you ready to do some serious camping?"

"Yes-I-am." Todd looked around the room. "Where's Mom?"

"Mom. Right. Well, the neatest thing happened, we met some old friends of your mom's, and when it was time to go she wanted to spend just a little more time with them. She'll be back in a day or two."

Jack could see alarms going off in Della's head and he winced. *This woman could spot a lie from the moon.*

Todd seemed content with the answer even if Della was not. "Can I put my stuff in your car, Jack?"

"Sure, bud. Go ahead. It's unlocked." Jack handed the duffel to Todd and held the door open for him, only to grab his shoulder as he tried to breeze through. "Whoa there a minute, pard. Don't you have something to say to Mrs. Kissinger?"

Todd spun around. "Uh, thank you for having me. See you, Kev." Then he was out the door.

Della smiled. "You sure you two aren't related somehow?"

Jack shook his head comically, and then turned toward Della's son. "It was great meeting you, Kevin. Maybe next time you're out here you can visit Todd at…" he tripped over his words, for he'd started to say "our house". Instead he finished with "his Mom's".

Kevin nodded, sad to see his new friend go. "We're Facebook friends."

"Right. Of course. You, uh, on Facebook, Della?"

"I don't even have a damned computer, Jack. But we have e-mail at work. I can write Kevin from there."

"I'm impressed." Jack started out the door. "Thanks again, Della."

When he saw that Kevin had retreated to the bedroom, Jack paused and scratched his head.

"So what really happened?" Della asked, her arms crossed.

"I'll let her tell you about it. She just needed a little more time, that's all. By the way, if she calls here looking for us, tell her I'm taking Todd to my place for the night."

"Gotcha. And if you need anything, anything at all

before she gets back, you just call on me, hear? And by the way, it's *Miss* Kissinger."

Jack nodded gratefully. "Right. Oh, and…here." He fumbled around in his pocket and withdrew a small trinket, dropping it into her outstretched hand. "It's also a pencil sharpener," he told her, and Della smiled, holding up the miniature Eiffel Tower as Jack hurried out the door to join Todd.

Todd took in Jack's model with awe. "Everything is so tiny, and so perfect! How did you do it?"

"With special, tiny, perfect tools. Wanna see?" Jack unfolded his set of Exacto knives, awls and saws. He stood by patiently while Todd experimented with each one, using scrap balsa wood from Jack's supplies.

"Then we paint it, lacquer it, light it if we want, and present it."

"What do they do with them after?"

"After what?"

"After they don't need them?"

"Oh, they pretty much get destroyed. By then everyone's touched it, picked at it, tried to change things that are glued down. *Were* glued down, I should say. They aren't much worth keeping."

"That's terrible. All that work."

"As long as I get paid, I don't care."

"But don't you feel like it's yours?"

"I'll tell you something Todd. Something I've learned about possessing things. You can't let them possess you. Sure, I possess this model right now. But what's more important, I possess the ability to build it. The set can and will go away, but not my skill as a model maker. At least I hope not."

"That's cool, Jack."

They ordered Chinese food and rented movies from the video store; after all, it was Friday night. They parked themselves on the couch, their shoeless feet propped on the coffee table. *I like this*, Jack thought, glancing over at Todd. *I hope we get the chance to do this again.*

He was in the kitchen getting refills of root beer for them both when the phone rang.

"This is Jack," he answered, unconsciously answering the way he did when he was working. "Um, hello?" he added.

There was someone on the line, but no words were spoken.

"Hello?" he said again, ready to hang up in another heartbeat.

"Jack. It's me."

"Well, the world traveler." Jack wet his lips, having found them suddenly dry at the sound of Maddie's voice. He waited for her next words.

"How are you?"

"Been better. I suppose you want to talk to Todd? He's here, in case you were worried."

"I wasn't worried. I knew he would be with you. And I would like to talk to him, when we're finished."

"Finished with what? Did we start something? I'm still not clear."

"Oh, Jack, please. I need to talk to you."

"I'm here. Come on over."

Maddie groaned in apparent frustration. Jack could hear her taking a deep breath before she spoke again. "You're still angry."

"Me? Naw. What's there to be angry about?"

"My being here. Letting you leave. I wish you hadn't."

Don't say it, Jack. For once, don't stick your foot in it.

Jack pressed his lips tightly together, walking across the room toward the couch. "It's your mom," he mouthed, handing the phone to Todd.

Todd's eyes lit, as Jack knew they would, and he growled inwardly. *She should be* here*, damn it*. He walked back to the kitchen and took a sip from his root beer, wishing it were something stronger.

As he watched Todd's face, his fever cooled. Happy, animated, Todd's youthful innocence touched his heart. The boy knew nothing of the turmoil that existed between them, nothing of the bizarre turn of events that had occurred halfway around the world. He also didn't know that his father was alive. His real father. What, Jack wondered, would that news do to Todd? Would he be happy, fearful? Confused, angry? Would he resent his father for staying "dead" so long?

Soon Todd beckoned; Maddie wanted to talk to him again. Jack sighed and took the phone, turning his back to Todd and returning to the kitchen.

"Okay. You don't have to say a word, obviously you are still upset and I guess I understand that," she began.

Her flippant tone set him off. "You guess? Do you have a clue about what happened to me over there?" His anger was quick to surface, molten and needing to be released at any opportunity.

"*You?* What about me? You can't possibly feel what I am feeling. The person I loved, worshipped, lived with, cared for, the person who took care of me, cherished me, honored me for eight years of my life, the person who was willing to die rather than put me through a torturous future is suddenly back in my life. I grieved for him, Jack, I grieved badly. I missed him. He was and is a generous and kind person. He's also Todd's father. Did you really expect me to just pat him on the head and say, that's nice you're alive and then leave?"

Maddie's words were hotly spoken; Jack was taken aback. So there *was* a bit of self-righteous, Irish temperament there. He wet his lips again and cleared his throat. "No." Jack rubbed his eyes, trying to envision Maddie in all her beauty, all her anger. "Key word there, 'expect.' How could I 'expect' anything? It wasn't exactly an everyday occurrence."

"Well I think you could have used a little more common sense maybe…a little compassion. What would you have done in my place?"

Boy, she wasn't about to let up on him. This was unreal, unpleasant, and only getting worse. "Look, Maddie, can we talk about this another time? Like when you come home? If…" he paused for effect, "you are coming home."

Jack could tell by her silence that his words had hit their target, stinging her painfully. He imagined that the tears were coming again, staining her beautiful face with permanent blue ink. He was instantly filled with remorse.

"Of course I am coming home." Her voice was small and barely audible. "The only question is whether Thomas is coming with me."

So there it was, the final blow. Slowly and carefully, Jack recradled the phone. He stared at it for several moments, his face contorted in confusion.

What just happened there? Wasn't I going to apologize?

He groaned to himself, and then returned to sit with Todd. After a moment's reflection, he slapped Todd on the back. "Hey, we'd better get busy and get that gear together." Jack attempted to clear his head, deciding he had better focus on the coming weekend. "It's in the loft, and I'm gonna need your help."

Together they climbed the stairs to the loft above the studio and dug around looking for the camping equipment

Jack had collected during his years with the forest service. Todd was excited about every new discovery.

"It sleeps three, and sets up in about five minutes," Jack was saying, handing the tent to Todd. "Here's the lantern…and somewhere here I have a propane stove."

"This is awesome. Wait'll Bryan sees all this cool stuff."

Jack grinned in the dim light. Todd's perpetual good mood was helpful, reminding him that things could be worse. What if Todd was a real brat, a delinquent, a moron?

They dusted and rechecked each item and placed it near the front door of the townhouse. Todd went digging into his school backpack for the flyer describing the trip.

"Says we hafta bring our own food for most of the time, but they're bringing hot dogs and sodas for the lunch on Sunday."

"Okay. Let's hit the store."

Neither Jack nor Todd slept well that night, Jack still agonizing over Maddie's suggestion that Thomas may accompany her home. Todd's anticipation of the beach trip had him wired. They rose early and ate doughnuts and cocoa for breakfast, then loaded the car and were off.

The beach campground was around eighty miles up the coast, and Jack cruised at a comfortable speed, in no real hurry. They talked about school, and college, and vocations. And then Todd asked Jack about *Jerry Maguire*.

"Remember in the beginning, when Jerry was, you know, with that woman?"

Jack squinted as he looked at the highway ahead. He hoped Todd wasn't asking about the scene he thought he was. "The old girlfriend?"

"Yeah, you know, where they're…doing it."

"Oh. That scene. Yeah." Jack swallowed. He could only imagine what the next question was going to be. Quickly he tried to remember at what age he'd become sexually aware of women, when his father sat down with him for "the talk."

"Why did Jerry do it with her? If he didn't love her?"

"Well, gee, I think Jerry *thought* he loved her…"

"Mom says people should never do it unless they love each other."

Jack coughed. Keeping the smile from his face was a task. This would be one of those moments of truth. "Well, she's pretty much right, Todd. For most people. I think some people, well, they just don't really…need to be in love, they just do it because…"

Todd looked at him expectantly.

"It feels good." *Yeah, that's it. That was safe. Surely the boy knows that much.*

"Like Ray?"

Jack turned to stare openly at Todd before tearing his eyes back to the road. "What? What's that supposed to mean?"

"Never mind."

"No, really. I think you may be thinking something wrong, bud. Ray loved your mom. They were just different, that's all."

Clearly, Todd wasn't satisfied. His silence said it all. Unsure how to respond to the situation, Jack said nothing more, waiting for Todd's next question. He didn't wait long.

"In the movies, people are doing it all the time."

"Hmm."

"Do people really do it all the time, Jack?"

God, I hope I'm not blushing, Jack thought as he nearly steered the Acura onto the shoulder. "I guess that depends on what you think is 'all the time'. People…men and women, when they love each other, being together feels really good, like the best feeling in the whole world. Whether it's just sitting together, or holding hands, or…*doing it,* they just do what feels good when they both feel like doing it." He stole a quick glance to see how his description was being received. Todd stared straight ahead.

"Like every night?" he finally asked.

We should be so lucky, pal, Jack wanted to say. It would still be a few years before he could share thoughts like that. "No, Todd. Not usually."

Jack waited a reasonable amount of time before changing the subject. He didn't want to appear to be avoiding Todd's very important questions. "So, you know most of the kids in your class? Anybody coming I should watch out for?"

"Sandy and Marla are coming. They giggle and whisper all the time. Makes me sick."

"Ah. Okay. I'll steer clear of those two."

"I'm not sure if Annie is coming."

"Annie? Another giggler?"

"No. She's real quiet. But weird."

"How so?" Jack was a lot more comfortable with this topic of conversation than the last.

"Well, she asked to borrow my eraser, but I know she has one of her own. I saw the teacher give her one. She put it in her pocket."

"That's pretty strange."

"Yeah, I thought so too. And another time she asked me if she could borrow a dollar for a candy bar. But she didn't even buy one. And she's always turning around and looking at me."

"Maybe you're being a bonehead."

Todd turned his head swiftly in Jack's direction. "What?

A bonehead? Why?"

"She probably likes you. I once knew a chick like that. They'll never come right out and tell us, they treat us like we're supposed to just know everything. It's weird. I mean, we're guys, darn it. We're simple. They're complicated. Sometimes I think they expect too much from us."

Jack chuckled to himself, and Todd laughed, too.

"Are you going to marry my mom?" the boy asked suddenly.

For the second time in ten minutes, Jack nearly ran the car aground. Lifting his eyebrows high, he sighed. "I'm not sure."

"You want to, don't you?"

Jack pondered just how honest he needed to be with Maddie's son. So much depended on what happened when she came home. He swallowed. "Yes. Yes, I do."

"Did you ask her?"

"No. Not yet."

"Are you going to?"

"What is this, the Spanish Inquisition?"

Todd smiled. "Just wondering."

"I'm not sure the time is right, pal. Your mom and me, well, to tell you the truth, we had a little argument. She's a bit pissed off at me right now. We need to talk things over when she gets home."

"Is that why she stayed? 'Cuz she's mad at you?"

"Partly."

"You shouldn't worry. She gets mad at me lots of times, but she always says, no matter how mad she gets, she will always still love me. She always forgives me. That makes me feel better. I hate it when she gets mad."

Jack nodded. He certainly shared that feeling.

"Just ask her. She'll say yes, I know she will. And then

you can live with us and be my dad for real."

A lump rose in Jack's throat at this unexpected admission. He reached across the seat and stroked Todd's hair, then tousled it. "I hope you're right. I'd like nothing better." Jack thought for a moment. "And you, I might add, may want to pay a little closer attention to a certain young lady. You may still be young enough to learn how not to be a bonehead!"

Fifteen

Jack stretched and looked out across the campground as families were busily erecting tents and opening ice chests. Todd had already run off with Bryan, their own tents being set up and their gear unpacked. The camp was on moderately wooded grounds, the sandy beach beginning roughly fifty yards away. Thirty or more sixth graders bounced around amongst the trees, their parents all trying to keep track of them. Jack wasn't worried.

That was the thing about Todd. You didn't need to worry about him most of the time. Responsible and well mannered. A kid any dad would be proud of.

It wasn't long before he spotted Todd again, running wild through the trees with his friend. He looked very young at the moment, much younger than his twelve years. Jack thought back to the ride that morning and the questions Todd asked. Shaking his head, he wondered what Maddie would say about them. Especially about she and Ray and their loveless sex.

The thought of Maddie brought with it a sigh. How he missed her! Missed the way she was before, before they had gone to Europe. Before Thomas climbed out of his empty grave.

After sunset, a great campfire was stoked and many of the families drew around it, sharing snacks and stories. Jack sat beside Todd on one of several huge logs that served as benches around the fire, and Jack tutored Todd on the proper method of roasting marshmallows.

"They get a little burned, but that's normal," Jack was saying, gingerly touching the charred and melted confection on the end of his stick. Realizing that Todd had not responded, he looked over to see Todd's gaze focused on something or someone on the opposite side of the circle. Meanwhile, his marshmallow was a bubbling black blob.

"Hey there buddy, I didn't mean *that* burned." Jack reached across and pulled Todd's stick away from the flames. Following the direction of Todd's stare, Jack noticed a young girl with a similarly comatose look.

Ah. Annie.

"Whadya say, Jack?"

"Uh, nothing. You just like yours well done, is that it?"

"Huh?"

"Never mind. Why don't you just invite her to sit with us?"

"What?"

"Hello…Earth to TJ…" Jack teased, spearing another marshmallow and dangling it over the campfire. He leaned closer to Todd, speaking softly. "Which one is she?"

"Who?"

"I thought we talked about this. How you're not going to be a blockhead anymore."

Todd frowned, then his face softened. Looking down, he spoke conspiratorially from the corner of his mouth. "Bonehead. Not blockhead. And...Pink shirt."

"Hmmm. Nice. Now get up and walk over there."

"What do I say?"

"Ask her…ask to borrow her eraser."

"Huh? That's dumb."

"Just kidding! Loosen up, dude. Ask her if she'd like to

take a walk tomorrow. To look for shells or something. Chicks dig that kind of stuff."

"She's not a chick, Jack."

"Sorry. I'm dating myself. Just do it."

Todd got up and moved in a haphazard way around the fire, first pretending to search for something in his pack, then waving at Bryan who was sitting near the intended female. As he passed her, he acted as if it were almost an afterthought and turned back to her, his eyes darting back to Jack's for support. Jack gave him a discreet "thumbs up."

Although he could not hear their words, Jack was charmed by the nonchalant way in which Todd approached the young girl. Suddenly, they were having a real conversation. Jack grinned and looked up at the stars. Well at least someone was getting "lucky" tonight.

"Did she say yes?" Jack asked later.

"She said she'd ask her dad. He brought her here."

"Good start."

They were settled into the tent for the night. In the near total darkness, Todd came up with another question or two that set Jack's mind reeling again. So this was what fathering was all about! He hoped he was answering the right way, the way Maddie would want him to. It made Jack feel important somehow, gave purpose to his growing relationship with Todd.

Jack was glad the darkness hid his smile from Todd as he recalled the time he'd asked his own father about his unexpected and embarrassing arousal during class, the involuntary erections and wet dreams. As the oldest, he'd later been called upon to teach his brother about such things. It was his duty as the first, his father had insisted. Now, Jack's heart was heavy with sympathy for the boy who'd gone twelve years without a real father. Todd had to be filled with many uncertainties and more questions. Silently, Jack hoped he would be around to answer them.

Todd tossed and turned beside him. Unable to get comfortable himself, Jack pondered Todd's worries about Annie, and the secret, un-talked about subjects Todd had shared with him. "So, Todd, did I ever tell you about the time I was mauled by a black bear?" Jack spoke in a comforting tone, hoping that a good story would put Todd to sleep.

"Were you really a forest ranger, Jack?"

"You bet. I was a cartographer. I drew maps of some of the parks up north. I also sketched plants and landmarks for their field guides. It was fun. Except for the night I got in between that ol' mama bear and her cub."

"You must have been scared!"

Not as scared as I am right now, Jack thought. He grimaced in the dark. Scary is not knowing how close you are to losing everything.

Sunday morning the whole gang met on the beach. The school principal, Mr. Laughlin, clad in Hawaiian shirt, Bermuda shorts and flip-flops, handed out mock diplomas and plastic leis to the sixth grade class of Liberty Elementary School. Immediately following the mock graduation, while the parents prepared the big weenie roast, a boom box was fired up with surf music and the kids scattered along the beach. Jack was handed a paper chef's hat and long handled tongs.

"You're the weenie turner."

Jack turned to face a large man with a goofy grin. Boasting the physique of a linebacker and the face of a maturing cherub, the man exuded friendliness and goodwill. His smile was genuine and Jack found himself grinning back as he opened the hat and slid it onto his head.

"My daughter seems quite taken with your son," the man was saying as he ripped open the first package of hot dogs. Startled, Jack had to grasp the paper hat as the wind caught it.

"Todd? Oh, he's not really-"

"Ready for girls? Neither am I." The man extended his hand. "I'm Len. Annie's been talking about Todd for weeks."

Jack nodded. "Jack. Yeah, I've never quite figured them out myself. I'm not much help. Have you seen Todd?"

Jack squinted toward the surf, his eyes keenly searching for Todd's red swim trunks.

"They took off looking for shells or something. They're okay." Len waived his arm in the direction of the beach.

Jack nodded. He felt another tinge of sympathy for young Todd, just beginning the roller coaster journey that would probably last his whole life.

The ride home was quiet, each of them absorbed by their own thoughts. Jack had been partly successful in blocking out his problems, but now as the dark highway before his headlights gave little distraction, his thoughts turned dark as well.

At home, nothing had changed. There was a call from Rick, his hockey buddy, with an invitation to a football game yesterday afternoon. An unexpected call from his mother, inquiring after his well-being. Apparently, the campground was a cellular dead zone. But no call from Maddie.

He made up the hide-a-bed for Todd and went to his room to get ready for bed. As he brushed his teeth, he knew he would not be able to sleep, so after putting on an old t-shirt, he went back to the living room, fired up his laptop and opened the browser. When the six familiar multi-colored letters appeared on the screen, he typed into the search bar. "Thomas LaForge."

Of course, there were numerous entries. Jack refined his search to a time period thirteen years before and was rewarded with a brief story about Thomas' disappearance during a storm. Jack frowned. There had to be more, so he continued to browse.

Page after page returned information on other LaForges. What had he been? A tutor? Nothing. What was his wife's name? Lily? Nothing. No property, no boating info, no memberships. On a whim, Jack added the city "Rochecarbon" to the search criteria, but still nothing came up. "This guy's a ghost," Jack muttered. Even though he considered himself a somewhat private person, Jack knew that a search on his own past would reveal a number of references: a hockey award in 2005, a car accident in '07, a mention of his forestry services in the Los Padres National Forest newsletter. At one time, he'd been listed as Duncan's father, but that entry had been removed. His work in the movie industry had netted him several film credits and a couple of top-shelf trophies. He was arrested for picketing once, but Jack wasn't sure it was online.

Thomas LaForge of Southern France did not exist beyond the day he was said to have died.

Maddie did not sleep alone. Unable to sleep at all, she stayed up half the night, sipping Cabernet and reacquainting herself with her former lover.

"What are you thinking, *chérie*? Your face is too sad."

"Oh, Papa, I feel like my life is…Jack calls it spinning out. I wish I knew what to do."

"Come." He beckoned to her, and she sat beside him

on the couch. Carefully he wrapped his arms around her, pulling her close against his broad chest. Maddie stiffened at first, but once her cheek settled against him she absorbed a sense of peace that had long evaded her. She closed her eyes. This was truly Papa.

"This is one of those times, Madeleine, when you must listen to your heart and no one else's. You must not think of what is right for me or Jack, or even our son. Because what is right for you will be right for Todd."

"I wish I could just stay in this spot for the next several weeks. Months. I just might, too, if I thought Todd would be okay."

Thomas stroked her hair away from her cheek, gently caressing her face with his large hands. "Todd is a fine, capable young man, and I could not be more proud. Even if he does not know I exist."

"He should know, Papa. He must know. I don't know how I can keep from telling him."

"It is your decision. You know what is best for your son. *Our* son. You cannot know how I regret not being there to watch him grow." His words struck a chord, an unpleasant one, for weren't those Jack's own sentiments about Duncan? His own fear that Duncan would be raised without his real father?

"Oh, Thomas, is it possible that Jack would go so far to see his son grow?"

"What do you mean, chérie?"

"She said he only wanted to marry me so he could get custody."

"She, who?"

"Elise."

Thomas grunted and shifted his weight beside her, and she sat upright. "That is nonsense. Oh, Elise! It angers me that she would hurt you so." He leaned close to her face, sliding his fingers into her hair and grasping her neck. "Madeleine, if only I could turn back the clock…" And with those words, Thomas kissed her full on the mouth.

Like Alice down the rabbit hole, Maddie began to fall. Backward, then forward, the gears and cogs of her internal time piece grinding and jamming. Dizzy, she pressed her face into his cheek and he embraced her. With her eyes closed, she tried to recall the twenty-six-year-old French tutor winking at her from the classroom door. Memories washed over her like small, recurrent waves at the beach, each bringing images she had long since locked away. His lips, so full and encompassing, the bristly feel of his mustache, the romantic French accent and elegant European charm…but no. Too many years, too much had passed.

Jack's words again came back to her, echoed in her head. *Father figure*. Bringing her fingers to her mouth, she slowly wiped the kiss from her lips.

Thomas released his grip. He pulled away, and in doing so his fingers closed on a chain; a silver chain, hanging around her neck, its charm well hidden inside her blouse. He plucked it out with one smooth movement.

"Ah. The Celtic knot. Am I correct that this is a gift from a liar? A man who could take away theatrical awards for his performance in my garden? Or is it from the man who would bring his woman around the world to the home of her long lost lover in order to ease her mind? The man who is, right now, kicking himself for leaving her there."

Maddie bit her lower lip. She was afraid to let herself believe that Thomas was right. She thought about the reasons Jack brought her to France, about the bank account and the painting.

"You never told me why you did it."

Thomas turned to peer into her face, his expression puzzled.

"Why you set up the money. Did you honestly think we wouldn't question the origin?"

"I have already admitted to being a fool. It was my happy expectation that the mystery would be a welcome one to a boy of Todd's age. Once, an anonymous benefactor was a complimentary, exciting occurrence!"

"Oh Papa, these days, in America, you just can't do things like that. People worry when strangers know too much about their children. At first, I thought they might be from Ray."

Thomas uttered a sound of disgust, and then sighed. "I suppose when Paul called and told me you were coming, I was not truly surprised. Fearful, yes. I was afraid that you would hate me for what I'd done. There is much you do not know about me. But, at last, I decided I deserved whatever happened. Perhaps, in my secret heart, I was hoping you would one day discover me and my deceit. Ultimately, even if you hated me, it would be better than living the lie."

Maddie was quiet while absorbing his words. She could never hate him for what he'd done out of love. Thomas had suffered as much, or more, than she.

"I've done some things in my life that I am not proud of. There are things...you do not need to know, not now. It's behind me now, and I hope it will stay that way. I suppose I thought that enough time had passed, that you might be saved from my past, innocent of all, and maybe we could pick up where we left off. What I did not expect was the depth of Jack's love for you." Thomas averted his eyes.

"So you believe that Jack truly loves me?"

"My darling, he is a man possessed by his love. It is obvious, not only to me, that you represent the end of Jack's search for true love. And when you emerge from this unfortunate storm of confusion I have created, you will realize that he, too, may be the end of your search."

Monday morning dawned too soon. Jack stared hard at the calendar on his kitchen wall, absently flipping hotcakes on a griddle. Behind him, Todd poured out two glasses of orange juice and carried them to the table, then returned for forks and knives.

"Man. I am *so* behind," Jack muttered, lifting the calendar page and looking into the next month. "I'll never get caught up." Murmuring under his breath, he stacked the pancakes on a plate and joined Todd at the table.

"Syrup?" Todd offered.

"Nope. I'll eat mine plain. Bacon?"

"Sure."

"How good are you at painting?"

"Okay, I guess," Todd answered. "You mean like a fence? Or a wall?"

"No. I mean like that monstrosity in there." Jack pointed toward the studio where the unfinished set model sat waiting. "We gotta finish that. Today."

Todd's eyes grew round at the thought that Jack would actually trust him to work on his masterpiece.

Jack was a patient teacher. Using tiny brushes and acrylic paints, Todd painstakingly painted miniature furniture pieces and military props. Jack, meanwhile, went back to affixing new pieces to the other side. It was a tedious, time-consuming job, but they worked companionably. Used to working alone, it was a pleasant change for Jack.

At five o'clock Jack called it finished. He'd lacquer it tomorrow, after all the paint was dry, but it was basically done. And not a bad job, either, he decided. The model would please the powers that be.

He was scrubbing the glue and paint from his fingers when the phone rang.

"Could you grab that?" he hollered to Todd, who was scouting the refrigerator for a snack. Todd reached for the cordless.

"Mom! You're home!" Todd's exuberance hit Jack like an icy draft against his back as he stood at the sink. He reached for a towel. It wasn't long before Todd handed him the phone.

"Yeah," he said casually, feeling suddenly like the phone itself was a foreign object, uncomfortable in his hand. "You're home?"

"Yes. I'd like to…to come and get Todd, if that's all right."

"Not necessary. I'll bring him home. Give me a few minutes to change."

"Thanks." Maddie paused for a moment. "Jack, Thomas is here." Her voice was firm; guarded.

"Peachy. See ya."

"Still mad, huh?" Todd asked as Jack burned rubber down the driveway.

Now mindful of his actions, Jack slowed the car down. "Looks that way."

"She said she brought me a surprise."

"Oh, yeah, that she did. A big one."

"You know what it is?"

"I think so."

"Will I like it?"

"Not sure, pal." Jack took a sideways glance at Todd. "Probably."

They parked in the street; Paul Adams had parked his

Cadillac in the driveway and was just getting into it when Jack and Todd arrived. Jack returned his wave curtly, and then opened the trunk to unload Todd's bags. Behind him, he could hear Maddie rushing out to greet her son.

Jack approached them slowly, appraising Maddie as she hugged Todd on the porch. She looked wonderful, he admitted to himself. A sight for sore eyes. And what sore eyes he had.

She saw him then, over Todd's shoulder. Her smile faded to a glimmer.

"Hello, Jack," she said, her voice breaking. "Come in."

Do I have to? And see him *again?*

He dropped Todd's things at the foot of the stairs and the three of them went into the living room.

"Where's my surprise?" Todd looked around anxiously. Jack followed his perusal of the empty room.

"TJ, I have to talk to you about something." Maddie nervously rubbed her palms together. She looked hesitant as she peered down the hall toward the guest room door.

"Maddie, do you really think this is a good idea?" Jack asked. "Maybe *we* could talk a little first?"

But before she could respond, the door opened and Thomas shuffled into the room.

Todd became uncharacteristically still. His lips parted in surprise, his eyes widened and his brow creased. He looked back at his mother, his face a picture of confusion.

"Todd." Maddie grasped her son's hands in hers, her voice quivering. "A long, long time ago, a terrible mistake was made. And even though it was that, a terrible mistake, it was made for a good reason." She glanced apprehensively at Jack, who first met her gaze and then looked away in disdain. After taking a deep breath, Maddie continued. "Your father did not drown in the ocean like we thought all these years.

Todd, are you listening? This is your father. This is Papa."

Todd looked back at the man standing before him. The man whose photo had been on the dresser for ten years. The man with dark eyes and bushy mustache and full eyebrows. The man was nodding his head.

The cry seemed to come from somewhere else, beginning small and growing to a wail by the time it reached his lips. And then Todd was fleeing, running toward the stairs, where he stopped and turned defiantly.

"*No!* He is *not* my father! My father is dead! Jack is going to be my father now!" The tragedy reflected on the boy's face burned into the eyes and hearts of all watching him.

"Well, that's just great. What a nice present to bring home," Jack muttered, his sarcasm a thin veil behind which he hid his own pain. Maddie, however, was incensed and her face showed it.

"Todd, wait," she called, following the youth up the stairs.

Jack decided he'd better leave, before his own anger grew too great. Nodding in Thomas' direction, he started for the door.

"Wait. I need to speak to you." Thomas leaned on his cane and beckoned to Jack, who returned.

"I'm not sure you have anything important enough for me to listen to," Jack said, crossing his arms. "Why did you come here, anyway?"

"I had to. For her sake. And because I needed to explain something to you, Jack."

"Oh please, spare me. You didn't travel all the way over here to talk to me. I may be a fool for her but I'm not stupid."

"I was not completely truthful about the disease that

left me thus," he began, motioning with his cane to his left leg. "It is more." Slowly and with obvious discomfort, he lowered himself to sit on the couch. "There is another part of me, the part of a man that, shall we say, is essential to his intimacy…"

Jack frowned. "Do I really need to hear this?"

"I could not ask Madeleine to stay in a marriage without the physical love she so deserves. It would have been wrong, and yet I knew she would never leave me. You have to understand that, Jack."

Jack said nothing. So the man had been rendered impotent at thirty-three years old. *What a crime*. And it was true; Maddie would have stayed until the end.

"I wouldn't wish that on my worst enemy," Jack finally said, looking around awkwardly and avoiding Thomas' eyes.

"And I'm not *that*, despite what you think," Thomas said quietly.

A noise outside drew their attention, and Jack opened the front door to see a small moving truck in the driveway. Ray Tyler was walking toward the garage with two day laborers in tow.

"Hey McKenzie," he called with a wave. "I'm just picking up a few things. Maddie around?"

Jack's teeth began to grind. *Could this day get any worse?* "She's busy," he answered, his tone non-committal.

"That's okay." He directed the men to load his skis and several packed boxes into the truck, and then approached Jack. He handed over an envelope. "These are my keys and my garage door opener. Make good use of them," he said with a smile that was both comical and disarming. He was apparently growing his hair long again, and the rakish grin was one a woman like Maddie could have fallen for, Jack decided.

"I'll give them to her."

"Who's that?" Ray wondered aloud, gesturing toward the man standing behind the screen door.

"Oh, just another of Maddie's ex's," Jack informed him. Ray shaded his eyes with his hand to get a better look.

"Tom? No way."

"Yup. The long absent, long dead, I might say, and he's brought tales of your sordid affairs."

"My *what*?"

"Well, she'd already found out about Elise. But the word is that there were others before her." At this point Jack cared little about what he said to Ray.

Ray's keen blue eyes were piercing as he turned them upon Jack. "Bullshit! Elise was the first. The only one. And *she* seduced *me*, the bitch." Ray shook his head, clearly upset by this news. And, having met Elise, Jack believed him. At least they agreed on one thing.

"Jack. I know what you must think of me. Frankly, it doesn't matter. But I really did care for Maddie. We met at a time when we both needed something, and we had our needs fulfilled. She's a wonderful girl, but she fell out of love first, believe me. I screwed up with Elise. I admit it. She came after me like a banshee and I was feeling needy." He looked away, apparently recalling his surprise at Elise's pursuit. "I never wanted to hurt Maddie. And if that guy in there is telling her lies about me, that's not fair. I never did it, I swear." He shook his head again, then looked at the truck where his hired help was locking the back.

"I gotta go. Paying by the hour, you know. Will you-will you tell her for me? Tell her I'm sorry, tell that asshole in there he's got the wrong guy. And tell Todd he can keep the TV. I'll send him a postcard from Chile."

Jack nodded and watched Ray slide into the driver's

seat of the truck. As quickly as he'd come, Ray was gone.

Jack took the envelope inside and dropped it onto the kitchen counter. Checking the fridge, he found a beer and opened it, draining it down.

Alas. I have become a soap opera character.

Almost as if she knew Ray had come and gone, Maddie appeared from upstairs. She approached Jack, her eyes dark and snapping with hostility.

"What did you say to Todd? How *could* you? How could you turn him away from his father like that? You must have said something to him, something cruel and…and mean about Thomas! Just because you can't understand…" Maddie's eyes fairly sparked as she verbally lashed out at Jack.

"You think he reacted that way because of something *I* said? You don't know him very well, do you?" He crushed the empty beer can in his hand.

"Of course I do. He's my son. I know exactly how he is. We share everything."

"I think not. I think you don't have a clue about Todd's state of mind right now. And I resent that you think I don't. But of course, you know all about the fact that he's been waking up in the morning with a hard-on and he's afraid you'll find out and take him to the doctor? And sure, you know that his young man's heart is bursting at the seams over a little doll named Annie? Yeah, you share *everything*. Even his concerns about you and Ray getting it on without being truly in love, right? Sorry I suggested otherwise."

"What are you talking about?" Maddie's face went ashen. "How *dare* you discuss sex with my child! Is this some kind of sick way of getting back at me for having loved someone before you?"

"Whoa. You hold it right there!" Jack shouted, tossing

the can into the sink and approaching her so quickly that she backed herself against the wall. Thomas, too, backed away, retreating to the kitchen.

"Have you forgotten who I am?" Jack began, his own eyes blazing with fury. "Have you? Seems to me you've suddenly forgotten everything. So let me remind you." His voice became low and deadly. "I am Jack McKenzie. I am thirty-seven years old; I was born and raised right here in this town. I am an honest man, a truthful man, I love my parents and I love children. I have a good job and the respect of my peers; I pay my taxes on time and I always take the shopping cart back to the front of the lot; but I am not perfect, and I like it that way. I sometimes drive too fast and I worry too much; I don't visit my folks often enough and my bank account is always out of balance. I have a deplorable temper and I have spent half my damned life trying to make it go away. And the worst thing I have ever done is cold cock my old man while he was beating the hell outa me."

He paused to take a breath, the anger still raging inside of him. Grasping her firmly by the shoulders, he spoke directly into her face. "It destroys me that you think I would meddle with TJ. I love that boy. And in case you've forgotten, I love you, too. Yeah, I'm the man who loves you. Me, damn it. I am cursed with this love. Do you need proof?"

With those words he pressed her against the wall, crashing his mouth against her lips painfully, assaulting her with a forceful and angry kiss.

Maddie's stunned expression made no impact on Jack. Her hands braced against his shoulders, she pushed Jack away with all her power, and then slapped him hard across the cheek.

"How *dare* you!"

"No. How dare *you*," he responded coldly, then turned

on his heel and walked brusquely out the door, ignoring Thomas who looked on in awe.

The door slammed behind him, but Jack could hear nothing, not even his own squealing tires as he sped away.

Sixteen

Todd sat at his desk, his fingers deftly cutting small pieces from the balsa wood scraps Jack had given him. The knife was old and not too sharp, but Todd's attention was rapt as he built the miniature table.

Maddie sat on the bed behind him, her hand grasping a tissue held to her mouth.

"Please talk to me, Todd. I never meant it to happen like this."

Todd didn't answer. Keeping his fingers busy, his mind focused, was the only way he could deal with what was happening. That was, not to deal with it at all. He believed with all his heart that Jack would return, Jack would fix everything and the man from the photo would go away. He and his mother would be happy again. For now, he would build the model and Jack would be proud.

Maddie stood and caressed her son's hair. "I'm sorry, darling. Please forgive me. I'll make everything right."

"Get Jack, Mom."

She bent and kissed Todd's forehead.

Maddie knew she had done Todd a great disservice, springing his real father on him without warning. And Jack, well, she'd alienated him for sure. But despite his rage, Jack was still saying he loved her. That was something.

Back downstairs, she poured a glass of wine for Thomas and herself. So peculiar, seeing him in her own home, sitting on the couch where Jack, and Ray before him, had sat looking at the TV.

"We never even owned a television when we were together," she mused. "We were too busy doing other things."

"True. Now, I watch it. It passes the time."

He seemed sad somehow, and Maddie again wondered at the wisdom of bringing him here. It had felt like the right thing to do in France. Phare de l'Ile now seemed a million miles away.

Some time passed before either spoke. Thomas drew in a deep breath, blinked several times and wet his lips. "You need to call Jack. This was all a mistake, and I am sorry."

"It's not all your fault. I should have—" Maddie's words were clipped by the sound of vehicles roaring into her driveway. She went to the window to find three black SUV's parked helter-skelter in front of the house and swarms of serious looking men rushing toward the front door.

"What is it?" Thomas called, now on his feet and leaning against his cane.

"Men in black," Maddie murmured. "They must have the wrong house." She responded to their knock on the door with dread knotting her stomach.

"Madelyn Tyler?" The first man asked, holding up an open wallet. "Joshua Knapp, FBI. We're looking for this man." The agent held up a four by six color photo of Thomas.

"Thomas LaForge. Is he here?"

Her lungs failed her. Unable to speak, she turned toward the living room just in time to see Thomas sprinting through the back sliding glass doors and across the yard, his abandoned cane askew on the floor. The FBI agents hurried past her in pursuit as Maddie flattened herself against the wall. Stunned beyond all reason, she watched as Thomas hurtled himself over the back fence and into the grassy pasture beyond.

"Ms. Tyler?"

Maddie gasped and returned her attention to an attractive young man peering into her face. "Are you all right?"

"No, I'm not all right. What do you want with Thomas? What's he done?"

An older agent approached, a cell phone pressed to his ear. "Okay... are you sure? Get 'em into the truck." The man slipped the phone into his pocket. "I'm sorry, Mrs. Tyler, but we'll need you to come, too."

Maddie frowned, then shook her head. "Not until you tell me what this is all about! Thomas is a guest in my home. What is he wanted for? Did you say your name was Knapp?"

"Yes, M'am. Mr. LaForge is wanted in France for the murder of Lillian LaForge, and there may be charges filed against you for aiding and abetting a felon. Now, you need to—"

"*What?* Are you joking? Thomas didn't kill his wife. She was hit by a car, or a bus or something. On her bike. In Tours. I've seen her grave."

"Did you see this accident occur?"

"Well, no, Thomas told me about it, though. And he's a very honest man." No sooner had the words left her tongue than Maddie was struck by the irony. Thomas LaForge was anything but an honest man. Tears stung her eyes. "If...if he really did something like that, I had no...no idea..."

Detective Knapp looked at the younger agent and blew out a breath. Maddie began to sob.

"Look, Mrs. Tyler, let's get downtown and sort this all out. You should probably make arrangements for your son."

"My son? You know about Todd? How...?"

"We've been watching you since you left De Gaulle."

Agent Carlson stayed while Maddie prepared Todd for a visit with Della. Her calls to Jack went unanswered.

"I got here as quickly as I could. You'll call me?" Della insisted, giving Maddie a quick hug. "Or have Jack get in touch?"

"If he ever responds. We...had words. Not sure where he's at, physically or emotionally."

"Everything will pan out, Mad. Don't you worry about TJ. We'll be great."

Maddie was seated under the glare of a fluorescent ceiling. Her eyes already burned from the ever-present tears threatening her eyes. Agent Carlson brought her a Styrofoam cup of water.

"Thank you. I'm just...I've never been so shocked about anything in my life. Well, I guess I was more shocked that he was even alive..."

Carlson sat down to continue the interview. "Now, you say you never met Mrs. LaForge?"

"No. Mrs.—Madame LaForge was already deceased when I met Thomas."

"I see. Now, in the five or so years you spent with Mr. LaForge, you had no knowledge of his position with the DGSE?"

"I don't even know what that is. Thomas was a tutor

and a translator when I met him. He tutored world political science. Later, he worked as a foreign correspondent for some news agency. But he was also a horticulturalist. And an artist."

"You never wondered about the many times he left town? Or the injuries he sustained while working?"

"His job took him away. And injuries? No. The only time he was ever sick or hurt was when he had cancer. Oh, and he once got hit by a loose jib on the boat."

The agent gave her a sympathetic smile. "I sincerely doubt this man ever had cancer, Ms. Tyler. And the injury to his left shoulder was rendered by a bullet he took while he was trying to steal documents from an American businessman in Paris."

Maddie pressed her hand over her mouth. Nausea welled up within her. How had she not known? Thomas, a spy? A wanted man? Could he possibly have killed Lillian? She reached for the water and took a sip, then cleared her throat. "How was he supposed to have killed his wife, if it's okay to ask?"

Agent Carlson looked around, as if making sure his co-workers were not witness to his breach. "He shot her when she threatened to expose his double agency. She was also with the DGSE."

"What is the DGSE, anyway?"

"The General Directorate for External Security. In French it's Direction Générale de la Sécurité Extérieure. France's external intelligence agency. It's operated under the French ministry of defense."

"Your French is very good," Maddie muttered. "So, who else was he working for?"

"Some rogue organization. I don't have those details. He's in interrogation now. He'll be extradited soon."

Maddie slumped back in the chair. "Are you going to arrest me, too?"

Agent Carlson smiled. "No. I'm reporting that you had no knowledge of the suspect's identity or history."

"Until last week, I'd thought him dead for thirteen years. I had a grave prepared for him and everything."

"Thirteen years? Wow. Uh, wow."

"Wow, what?"

"Madame LaForge was...uh, murdered just nine years ago."

Maddie leaned forward and placed her hand on the desk. "That's impossible. She was already dead when we were together."

"Did he tell you she was dead?"

"Yes!" Her heart racing, Maddie fought to remember the day Thomas told her about Lilly. "How is it that you guys are just now arresting him?"

"We didn't know where he was until you looked him up. But this investigation has been ongoing for many years. Madame LaForge was an American citizen."

"So you've been watching me all these years."

Agent Carlson looked away, then down at the file on the desk. "In some manner, yes. You're on a list to be flagged if you fly to Europe."

"I...don't know what to say."

"Well, we're done here. I'll get someone to give you a lift home. Here's my card, if anything comes up you think we should know, okay?"

"Okay. And don't leave town, right?"

"You got it."

"Can I see him?"

The agent looked uncomfortable. "I'll check. Wait here."

Thomas was handcuffed to the table. Maddie sat down opposite him, her eyes dry and her face calm. She stared at him, wondering just what she should or could say. He spoke first.

"It's all true, Madeleine. I've worked in counter-intelligence most of my life."

Maddie nodded slowly. "Must feel odd, lying every minute of every day? Disgracing those who love you?"

"I didn't kill Lillian. But I could not pursue her killer without exposing myself. It was easier to just bury her and move on. I exacted revenge in my own way. You do not want or need to know about that."

"I don't want to know anything about you, Thomas. I wish I'd never met you. Aside from Todd, you have given me nothing but grief, now."

Thomas lowered his chin, turned his wrists within the cuffs. "There is one thing I never lied about. I loved you, ma Chérie, with all of my being. Which is exactly why I left you when I did. Things were heating up. Your life was in danger, and that is the truth. The only way I could protect you, and ultimately, our son, was to create this elaborate charade. I didn't want to go, believe me.

"Earlier this year, I received more threats. I feared for my own life. That is when I set up the trust for Todd. If Elise had not sent that stupid painting, none of this would have happened."

Maddie took a moment to peer into Thomas' eyes. Was he finally telling the truth? "They told me Lilly was alive the whole time we were together. Is that true? Did you still have a wife in France while we lived there, and here? Is that why we never married?"

"Lillian and I never loved. It was a marriage of

convenience. We were both in the same...business. Part of our cover. When I met you, I wanted to live that normal life that had never been mine. And we succeeded, didn't we, for a time?"

Maddie couldn't answer. His charisma still shook her, and she feared she would buy into his treachery again. "I have to go. I wish you whatever is right."

"Where is Jack? Did he return after your disagreement?"

"I have no idea where he is."

"You will find him. Go."

Maddie shook her head. "Because of you, I have probably hurt the one man in my life that's been completely honest and forthright. The one man who truly plays on my team, who's been there for me through all this utter bullshit."

"You can fix this. He loves you." Thomas tried to reach for her hand but the handcuffs restricted his movement. "I wish you the best, my love. I know all the apologies in the world can't repair the damage I've done. Please, one day, try to forgive me and know that what I did, I did to protect you."

Todd was sleeping when she got home. Maddie gave Della the abbreviated version of what had happened, and her friend graciously did not press. She did, however, insist on staying the night. Maddie was too wasted to argue.

Jack had neither called nor stopped by. She'd left numerous messages on his phone, and at this point there was not much left to say. At eleven, she went to her room and lay down without undressing. She tried to sleep, tried to put the events of the past week out of her mind, all to no avail. She touched her lip and winced. The evidence of Jack's harsh attack on her mouth still stung.

Alternately she cursed him and defended him. She

drove him to it, she knew. Jack's revelations about Todd hurt her, and she wanted to hurt him back, then. Now all she yearned to do was curl up in his arms and make everything else go away.

At midnight she picked up the phone and dialed Jack's home number. His machine answered brightly.

"It's Jack, I'm either on the table or under it, so leave a message."

Maddie smiled a melancholy smile. When had she last heard him sound happy? Their first night in Paris, they laughed about the aphrodisiac qualities of oysters, and she had playfully moved the plate away from him.

She didn't leave a message. Instead, she hastily put on her shoes and socks and left her room. She peeked in at Todd, asleep in his bed. Careful not to wake him, she pulled his covers up over his shoulder.

She was surprised to see Della still sitting on the couch, a fresh glass of beer in her hand as she channel surfed the late-night television offerings.

"Oh, gracious. Why aren't you in bed? Is everything all right?"

"Yes. But I can't sleep. I'm going out."

"Well, listening to your heart can surely keep you awake. Be careful. I hope you find him."

Of course, Jack's townhouse was buttoned up tightly with no sign of Jack. She could see through the small garage window that his car was gone. At a loss, she got back into her truck and locked the doors, pushing the seat back to wait. It was 1:00 a.m.

What would she do and say when she saw him? Would he forgive her this last, meaningless confrontation? Oh, it was all too painful. She closed her eyes. The jetlag was bad enough without the glass of wine and the exhausting interrogation. Fatigue battered her until she finally gave in to sleep.

She was out for over three hours. Maddie wasn't sure what it was that woke her, a distant siren perhaps or the barking of a dog across the street. Her eyes quickly sought the dashboard clock; the green glowing digits read 4:30. A thick June fog crept in around her, and she decided to go home.

The streets were basically deserted this Tuesday morning. The headlights she saw in the fog were few and far between. She drove unconsciously, weary and disoriented, hoping her truck knew the way home. Neon lights left on overnight touting businesses that were closed glowed dimly along the sides of the boulevard. One gained her attention in particular. The familiar peacock logo of NBC.

One quick glance down the side street bordering the studio caused her to apply the brakes in the middle of the street. Luckily, no other cars were currently approaching, and she made a hasty U-turn mid-block. She turned down the side street and took a closer look.

The Acura was unoccupied. She pulled close to the curb and parked behind Jack's car, her heart beating a staccato rhythm in her chest. She turned off the engine and got out of the truck.

The fog was thicker here, sitting on the park like a cluster of fallen clouds. And while the faintest glow painted the horizon, the park still rested in darkness.

Hesitantly, she began her trek into the park, mentally "feeling her way" to the bench.

Jack was there, of course. She stopped short at the sight of his silhouette, lit briefly by the lights of a passing car. Sitting cross-legged on the bench, his chin rested on his fisted hands. She resumed her approach, walking until she was nearly touching him.

Maddie closed her eyes. She no longer worried about what to say. Her fingers went into his hair, her fingertips tracing their way across his scalp, luxuriating in the fall of his hair across her hands. Gently she pulled his head against the softness of her belly, and then slowly she knelt until she was looking up at his face. The grass was cold and wet, soaking into her tennis shoes and the knees of her jeans. She barely noticed.

The black T-shirt left his arms bare, but Jack was still warm to Maddie's touch. Lovingly she caressed him, feeling the hardened muscles, the hair on his arms, the strength in his wrists and hands. A tiny gasp escaped her throat at the sight of the bleeding knuckles on his right hand. And then she peered into his eyes.

For just a moment, all movement stopped. No cars passed by, no night birds flew. Even the fog seemed to have frozen around them, a billowy, cloistering cushion protecting them from the world. The feeling returned, the same feeling, the connection they'd made on this very bench so long ago. Jack's eyes no longer reflected wrath, only uncertainty and wariness wrestling with love. Love that was painful but true.

Maddie touched his lips with her fingers, and then bravely forced her own lips to speak.

"I-I wanted to tell you, I remember who you are."

"Who am I?" he whispered hoarsely.

"You are Jack McKenzie. You are the one I trust, the one I believe in. You are the man I want to wake up beside, every day of my life. You are the man I want to be the father of my children, all my children. You are the man I love, with all my heart, and all my soul, and everything in between."

She began planting planted tiny kisses on his bruised

fingers, but he stole her lips away with his own. Sliding off the bench, Jack knelt with her and took her into his arms, his true passion renewed. And with the end of that one very significant kiss, he stood and lifted her into his arms and carried her to his car.

Neither spoke a word until they reached Jack's house. He again carried Maddie, this time to his bedroom and lay her down on his unmade bed, climbing on top of her and sitting to unbutton her shirt. Purposefully he stripped away the layers of clothes that came between them.

Now both naked, they lay side by side in the growing light of dawn. Jack seemed interested only in caressing and stroking her body in long, unhurried movements. After a time, Maddie spoke.

"Why did you take off my clothes if you're not going to make love to me?"

"Who said I'm not?"

He touched her forehead, then dragged his fingertip down her nose, over her lips, down her chin into the soft recess of her throat, then slowly over her chest and between her breasts, finally catching on the silver chain that she still wore.

"This is the ultimate honesty," he murmured.

"It's getting light out. Do you want me to close the blinds?" she asked, preparing to get up.

Jack's hand was swift to hold her in place.

"No. The light is good. We've had too much darkness already."

Turning her head to one side, Maddie looked for the top sheet or blanket to cover her nakedness, only to find that Jack had tossed all of the covers to the floor.

"I'm cold," she lied, trying to reach over the side of the bed.

Again he stopped her, pulling her close against him. He continued to take his time, touching, tickling, exploring as Maddie squirmed and grasped at his hand.

Jack gave her a half-smile. "Do you know how it's been this past week?"

"How what's been, exactly?"

"My life. It's been some of the best, and some of the worst times I've ever had. This whole experience has really made me think about what I want, and what I don't want." Jack spoke softly and with great conviction.

Maddie wasn't sure how to respond. The room was now filled with sunlight, and she forced herself to ignore her modesty. Jack seemed unaffected by her nudity, despite the fact that he persisted with the finger play.

"Just when you think you know all you need to know about someone, something comes along and changes everything. I didn't want it to change. I wanted everything to stay rolling smoothly along. Then when things started happening, I blew it."

"*You* blew it?" Maddie asked, ready to shoulder the blame for all their problems.

"Sure I did. I made a commitment to you. And then I got my nose tweaked and I ran away. I apologize to you for that."

Maddie took a deep breath.

"You had no way of knowing…"

"It shouldn't matter. There were a lot of things I didn't know. I made assumptions based on my own fears. I made assumptions about you, and about Thomas. Even about Ray. I was wrong on all accounts, and I am amazed that I would put our relationship in jeopardy."

"Jack," Maddie began, sliding her fingernails through the hair on his chest and all the way up to his ear. "You can't possibly blame yourself for all that happened. I spent hours and hours over there, chastising myself for letting you go home alone. For letting that awful woman say those things about us. So many lies."

"It's in the past." His eyes were warm and loving, with just a hint of melancholy. He didn't seem altered at all by what she was saying, letting his eyes travel the length of her and back to her face, where he placed his palm on her cheek.

"And you were right about Thomas, he—"

"You are so beautiful."

Her modesty renewed, Maddie colored. "But you don't know what happened. Thomas, they came and took him, because he—"

"Shhh." Jack lifted himself to lie atop her, grasping her hands and pressing them into the bed above her head. "You really don't like this daylight stuff, do you?" he asked, clearly amused by Maddie's discomfort.

"Don't be silly. It's only natural."

"You liar. You may still have many secrets I've yet to uncover, but this isn't one of them."

Still embarrassed by Jack's bold appraisal, Maddie averted her eyes, giving him the opportunity to nuzzle her ear affectionately. Her body rebounded with shivers stronger than any chill could create, causing her to arch against him.

"Still cold, huh?" He peered down at her with a mischievous grin.

"Sort of." Looking back into his eyes, Maddie found his gaze inescapable. His power over her complete, she succumbed to his will and forgot about her nakedness in the morning sun. She forgot about the tears, the insecurities, the deceptions. She let go of the worry, the unknown path leading to tomorrow. She realized what the dawn meant to Jack, about dispelling the darkness and shadows that had grown between them. And she knew with a comforting certainty that all that had happened had happened for a reason.

"Everything's really going to be okay isn't it?" she whispered.

With just a touch of the devil still in his smile, Jack whispered back, "Probably."

His battle to keep from becoming aroused was lost, and Jack allowed his restrained passion to go free. Feeling that he came close to losing the best love he'd ever known gave more reason, more worth to his ability to conjoin with Maddie. More important now than even the first time, his need to reaffirm his commitment drove his passion to new heights.

And Jack was to discover that Maddie had no trouble being the recipient of that passion. Her own romantic agenda certainly included the need to prove that she belonged to Jack and only to Jack; to dispel his fears that there could ever be anyone else.

They were all over the bed, neither seeming to get enough of the other. Laughing, playing, delighting each other with a new confidence, enjoying the thick, sweet lust of new love.

When they were at last sated, content in the exchange of physical gifts and radiating in the afterglow of their pleasure, Maddie laid her head on Jack's shoulder. He finally retrieved the discarded sheet from the floor and tucked it cozily around her.

"Well, I'm spent," he murmured, closing his eyes.

Maddie was quiet, and Jack turned to see if she was sleeping. He found her staring at the ceiling, deep in thought.

"What's on your mind, my love?"

"I was wondering about those 'best times' you mentioned earlier. What were they?"

"The time I spent with Todd."

Maddie smiled. "I was hoping you'd say that. Did he really say all that stuff?"

"That and more." Jack chuckled. "He's just at that brink. He'll get through it." He paused to remember again his conversations with Todd. "It was a real eye-opener for me, though. Kids can fool you, I guess. He seemed like such a little kid before."

"What did he say…about me and Ray?"

Jack shook his head. "He said you told him people shouldn't have sex if they don't love each other, but he's noticed that people sometimes do, so he wanted to know why, and I said, well, because, ah, it feels good."

"Oh God."

"And that's when he said, 'like Ray.' I assured him, of course, that Ray did love you."

Maddie swallowed. "I just can't imagine him talking about my sex life! Thank you," she said softly, now closing her own eyes, "for being there for him. It means everything to me."

Jack nodded, but fatigue settled on him like the fog the night before, and soon the two of them passed into a deep, restful sleep.

Todd tumbled out of bed and ran for the bathroom. It was several moments before his discomfort dissipated and he could urinate. He brushed his teeth calmly, no longer panicked since his talk with Jack.

Back in his room he dressed quickly, then took a moment to examine his tiny table. It was perfect, he knew. The painful experiences of the day before seemed like nothing more than a bad nightmare, one he hoped was really over. He bounded down the stairs looking for his mother. What he found instead gave him pause. Jack was sitting in the kitchen reading the morning paper.

"Jack! You're here!"

"Hey, sport. Want some breakfast?

Jack watched as Todd went about getting his own juice and toaster waffle.

"Where's Mom?"

"She just went down to the market for a couple of things. I'm kinda glad because I wanted to talk to you, you know, without Mom here."

Todd brought his breakfast to the table and sat down across from Jack. "Okay, shoot."

"Shoot? Man. Okay. Well, first off, I want to apologize for losing it yesterday. I just sort of went off, and it was wrong. So, can you just kind of erase that from memory? I don't want you to, you know, use it against me in the future."

Todd smiled. "I just might have to."

"Fair enough."

"You were right to be mad, Jack. Mom was being stupid."

"Never. Your mom is never stupid. Misguided, maybe. And that's the other thing I want to talk about."

"That man?"

"He's your father, Dude. And like it or not, you can't change that fact."

"I don't like it."

"Well, that's your choice, and I understand it. But here's the dealio. Thomas has some bad times ahead of him, because he got into some deep doo-doo over in France. They're taking him back over there to determine if he's really bad-bad or just a little bad."

Todd nodded, then stuffed a forkful of waffle into his mouth.

"Now Thomas, you see, is still kind of a sentimental schlub. He knows he might have to, uh, go away, for a very long time."

"They're gonna throw him in the Big House?"

"Maybe. So, he's asked your mom if he can see you one more time before he goes. It's entirely up to you, Teej. You're a big guy now, and I trust you to make your own decisions about stuff like this."

Todd's chewing slowed and he did not meet Jack's eyes. "What if I say no?"

"That would be fine. No questions asked. You don't owe Thomas anything."

"What if I say yes? What happens?"

"You get to see the inside of LAPD. The FBI is holding him there. You would get to talk to him, or listen to him, as the case may be, for about fifteen minutes."

"What's he gonna say to me?"

"Oh, you know—I'm sorry, I'm a bad father, I wish I was a better guy, but I'm a crappy person, try not to hate me, take care of your mom—that kind of stuff."

Todd smiled briefly. "Alone?"

"No. Your mom or I would be with you."

He was wearing a plaid flannel shirt and a pair of thick glasses perched on his nose. Thomas looked up when Todd entered the room.

"Good morning, Monsieur LaForge. *Café noir, ou avec le lait*?"

"Huh?" Todd puzzled.

Thomas pulled the glasses from his face. "You drink

coffee, yes? Black or with milk?"

"No, yuck! I've already had juice, thanks."

"Ah, *oui*." Thomas looked down at the table, giving Todd the opportunity to stare at him some more. "Just juice?"

"No. I had a toaster waffle, too."

"Is this the usual breakfast of American children now?" Thomas asked, trying to hide his disdain.

"Not always. On the weekends Mom makes us bacon and eggs and French toast. Jack makes great pancakes, too."

"Ah. Good. I am glad to hear you get some nutrition. At home, Monique is filling our plates with fresh baked croissants, fruit from our little orchard, seafood she has bought at the market in Tours. She is even now canning and storing up the apricots that are ripening in the yard."

"Oh." Todd tried to picture such abundance of fresh food on the table every day. "Who is Monique?" he finally asked.

"Monique," Thomas began, his eyes shining merriment into Todd's serious ones, "is your sister. Your half-sister."

"My sister? I have a sister in France?"

"Yes. She is a lovely person. And she has two little girls, Jeanne and Nicole, who are five years old. They are your nieces."

"I'm an uncle, too?"

"*Certainement.*"

Todd was speechless. This was clearly a turn that he had not expected.

"Perhaps one day, you will meet them. They are anxious to meet you, Todd."

It was the first time the man had uttered his name. Todd managed a brief smile. "Do you have any animals?"

"*Oui*. We have chickens and a dog or two running outside. Some cats as well. And of course many animals drink from our river."

"You have your own river? Wow."

"It is not really *our* river. It belongs to the earth. To everyone. Only a small portion of its beauty belongs to us, in here," he said, pointing to his eyes.

Todd pondered the conversation and his father. There was a question lurking, a question that needed voicing, but Todd was hesitant. Finally, unable to contain himself, his lips began to move. "How come everyone thought you were…dead?"

Thomas LaForge sighed. From the day he left the lighthouse in Brittany until this very moment he had known the question would come, and he was actually relieved it had been uttered. Now, sitting across from the boy he had so longed to meet, he spoke the words he had practiced again and again.

"There was a terrible storm. I'm sure your mother has shared this part of the story with you. I was sailing the "Jeune Fille," my beautiful sailing vessel, and I made a wrong turn. Tremendous waves appeared, and great rushes of rain and wind pounded down upon my Fille. She could not hold. We went down, together."

Todd's eyes were wide in unabashed awe.

"I thought I would die. Indeed, I was near dead when a stranger picked me up and revived me. I was taken by a mysterious illness that affected my very thoughts. I somehow found myself back in France, thanks to some ill-advised but well intentioned friends."

"But why didn't you come back?"

"Ah, that is the question. By the time I was coherent and recovering, it was a long time later. Your mother had grieved long and hard at my passing and had finally met another, so I found out. I could not bear to disturb her happiness a second time. Right or wrong, I remained in France."

"Wow. That's awful. You must have missed her a lot."

"I did, my son. I did. But I was willing to live without her rather than cause her more pain."

"But she found you again. With Jack's help."

"*Oui*." Thomas risked a pat to Todd's arm. "You like this Jack, *non*?"

"Yeah. He's great."

Thomas thought he could see a glimmer of new respect in Todd's eyes. Perhaps Jack was the catalyst. The link. "He is right for your mama, make no mistake."

"They're saying you might go to prison."

"This is true. I made some serious mistakes when I was younger. Some things I didn't want to do. I will take whatever punishment is handed out. But someday, when this is all behind us, I hope you will come and visit us."

"Maybe," Todd murmured. "So, uh, good luck and all."

"He told me the big lie," Todd said in car on the way home. "About the boat and almost drowning."

"It's what he thought was best. He thinks you're still too young to know the truth," Maddie explained. "He also knows I'll be telling you the whole story. Doesn't matter now."

"He wasn't so bad, Mom."

Maddie looked across to Jack, who steered the car onto the freeway.

"Nobody's perfect. Thomas has a lot of repenting to do over the next few years. He has money, a good attorney, and maybe he'll beat the worst of the charges."

"Hmm." Maddie crossed her arms. "Not sure how I

feel about that."

The three spent the rest of the day quietly. After proudly showing Jack his mini-table, Todd uncharacteristically pulled out a novel and lay down to read. Maddie caught up on laundry while Jack made some preliminary sketches of an upcoming project. They made a simple dinner together, and afterward watched television until late. Maddie yawned.

"Time for bed?" Jack asked, eyebrows lifted in innocence.

"You're staying?"

"Thought I might."

Maddie threw her arms around his neck and held him close. Then she led him upstairs. For a fleeting moment, she worried that Jack might feel awkward sharing her bed, the same bed originally occupied by Ray. But soon the garments were flying off and the bed simply became a soft surface beneath them.

This time, their lovemaking took on a more romantic tone, Maddie thought. Jack whispered sweet words and made gentle overtures. The lights were dimmed but still on, and Maddie found she liked seeing his eyes, so filled with love and devotion. She did her best to reciprocate.

They showered the evidence of their pleasure from their bodies, discovering even new delights with a bar of soap in their hands. Their troubles running off like the bubbles down the drain, Maddie and Jack found new joys and plans to make.

With the light of a new day streaming in, Maddie stretched and got out of bed. "I kinda like hearing you sing in there," she called.

"What are you talking about?" Jack called back from the bathroom where he was shaving.

"Oh Jack," she said, rushing in to stand behind him and wrapping her arms around his waist. Pressing her cheek against his bare back, she kissed him, then peeked around to see his face in the mirror.

"Move in with me. Right now. Let's go pack it all up."

"What?" Jack looked alarmed.

"Let's do it. Move in with me and Todd."

Jack grabbed a towel and wiped the remaining traces of shaving cream from his face. Embracing Maddie, he smiled down at her. She traced the dimples around his mouth lovingly with her finger.

"We'll talk about that," he said softly. "One thing at a time. There's still a lot of unfinished business hanging around."

He was right, of course. Leaning down, he whispered into her ear, rekindling that familiar thrill throughout her body. "Like whether or not you want to marry me. I may not be, after all, an unconventional person looking for an unconventional relationship."

Epilogue

Todd walked beside the minister to the gazebo, fingering the simple gold and diamond band in his pocket. Seemed weird, somehow, to be attending his mother's wedding, to have her ring in his own pocket. The ring Jack had given him that morning for safekeeping.

He met Jack there. Jack shifted his weight from one leg to the other, alternately serious and grinning. Todd patted his breast pocket, acknowledging its contents to Jack, who squeezed Todd's forearm in return.

A smattering of folding chairs had been set up in the garden surrounding the gazebo. The Palm Springs sun, uncharacteristically mild, shown down on the guests: Jack's parents; Sean and his girlfriend-of-the-month; his cousin Case and his pal Matt; and friends of the McKenzie family from neighboring homes. Della looked smug, but lovely, her copper hair blazing against the turquoise sky. Two-year-old Duncan squirmed on her lap, his sunny smile nearly bringing tears to Jack's eyes. Paul Adams and his wife sat on one end, holding hands. Paul said something to her and then returned to the house.

"Are you nervous, Jack?" Todd whispered.

Jack turned to his stepson-to-be. "What do you think?" He held his shaking hands out before Todd's eyes. "Can't figure why, though." He leaned comically to the side, bumping into Todd's shoulder, which, he noticed, was now nearing his own in height. Todd had really shot up in the past year.

"Yeah, it's only Mom," Todd reminded him.

"Hmm. Only Mom." Jack's voice noticeably softened as his eyes fixed on his parents' back door.

Music began wafting from the open windows in the living room; piano music, playing the preamble to the wedding march. The door opened and the twins came tumbling out, each with a small basket of rose petals they were to drop in the bride's path. Of course, they threw the petals by the handfuls, prompting giggles and smiles from the onlookers.

Next, Monique was on the swath of white carpet, her face bearing a Mona Lisa smile. Unhurried, her eyes played across the faces of the onlookers, and her younger brother standing in the gazebo. She winked subtly at Jack, whose already heightened emotions colored his cheeks. And upon reaching them, she gave both Todd and Jack a kiss on the cheek before standing to one side.

The music stopped briefly, and all eyes were tuned on the porch. Jack's lungs filled and froze; he felt like he might never be able to breathe again. He did, of course, exhale at the sight of his bride emerging from the house, carefully escorted by Paul Adams.

They had kept Jack from seeing Maddie, honoring the age-old tradition. Bad luck, Monique had insisted. Great pains were taken for her to use the front entrance to the house, Jack using the side ones. And when they'd almost met in the hall this morning, Monique hastily threw a towel over Maddie's head, laughing at Jack's mock chagrin.

It was the first night she had not slept beside him in

nearly a year. And now the sight of her strolling slowly down the bridal path toward him turned his insides into jelly.

Maddie wore no veil, a simple rose and ribbon headdress giving her dress a storybook quality. Indeed, she might have walked straight out of Anderson's Fairy Tales, Jack thought, unable to keep the smile from his lips.

The simple yet romantic gown was fetching. The modest swell of her belly beneath the high waist added to her aura, for what could be more feminine than the sleeping form of their unborn child?

By the time she reached him, Jack was ready to pitch the entire ceremony and run off with her across the verdant golf course behind the McKenzie property. In his mind's eye, he would also be tearing away his tie and vest!

Maddie viewed the gazebo ahead of her, hoping she could hold back her tears long enough to get a clear view of the happy-faced minister, her beloved son and her—oh my God!—drop-dead-gorgeous husband-to-be. She fleetingly wondered how she had come to this day; how she could possible deserve the happiness that filled her.

They walked slowly, for Maddie didn't want the moment to pass too quickly. Just before leaving the parlor, Paul had kissed her cheek, and then pressed his own against it.

"I wish you all the happiness in the world, Maddie. Truly."

"Don't you dare make me cry, Paul," she responded, giving his chin a little pinch.

"Tears of joy are lucky," he said, taking a pinkie to the corner of his own eye.

And now she stepped into the gazebo and took her betrothed's hand. After bestowing a warm smile upon her son, her eyes met with Jack's and did not leave them.

The minister opened his worn, black leather book of praise, turning the pages to those most often read. Reciting the words more from memory than from sight, he blessed the bride and groom and their family-to-be. Their vows were simple yet powerful, a reaffirmation of those already exchanged between them.

Paul cleared his throat when the question was posed. "I give this woman," he announced clearly and passionately, then stepped out of the gazebo and sat in the vacant chair waiting beside his wife.

"May we have the rings?"

Transfixed, Todd watched his sister wrestle Jack's ring from her middle finger and hand it over to Maddie. Jack nudged him gently.

"Sorry!" he whispered, fishing the tiny band from his pocket and pressing it into Jack's palm.

"It's okay, pal," Jack said, calm now and in control. He accepted Maddie's ring, then gently slipped the gold band onto her finger beside the diamond engagement ring she already wore.

"Wow," Maddie said with a giggle, pressing her left hand against her tummy and staring down at it.

"What it is?" Jack asked.

"He's turning cartwheels!"

The minister smiled patiently, and those guests near enough to hear the exchange chuckled. Monique grasped the bride's right hand affectionately.

Maddie held Jack's hand against her tummy as they completed their vows. The minister was joyous when he could finally pronounce them husband and wife, and Jack pulled his bride close for the kiss everyone waited to see.

The scent of magnolias swirled about them. Unmindful

of the on-lookers, they kissed one another hungrily, intimately, each infused with desire. It took all the strength Maddie could gather to pull her lips from his and turn to acknowledge the applause of their friends and well-wishers.

Maddie felt she was watching herself from another place. She peered into the bright summer sky, spying a magnificent bird circling the heavens above. Around and around he flew in celebration, and Maddie sensed a closure. A full circle had finally met its beginning, and would forevermore be complete. A circle made of two who loved with all their hearts, their souls, ever and always.

THE END

MEET ANNE CARTER

"Everyone needs a little romance in their lives," Anne Carter will assure you. "Some need more than others." She should know. A storyteller since 7th grade, Anne and her younger sister would dream up a new chapter to a romantic saga each night before going to bed. Soon, writing became an obsession. Raised in Southern California where she, her husband and three children make their home, Anne interrupts her passion occasionally to run her bookkeeping business and possibly put dinner on the table.

"***Ever & Always*** began as a novella called *In Too Deep,* detailing Jack & Maddie's history and courtship. Jack McKenzie went on to appear as a supporting character in *Point Surrender* and *Cape Seduction* of the Beacon Point Romance Series. Finally, Jack gets his own romantic suspense in *Angel's Gate*. With the completion of *Angel's Gate*, it was obvious that Jack's fans would want more of his backstory, so *In Too Deep* was ramped up and reformed as *Ever & Always*."

Next in the series: Point Surrender

Visit Anne at http://www.anne-carter.com.

ALSO BY ANNE CARTER

Paulie & Kate's Story:

Unmasking Paulie Bingham
For the Love of Katrina Bingham

StarCrossed Romances (Series):

StarCrossed Hearts
A Hero's Promise
The Gypsy in Me (Fall, 2014)

Beacon Point Romances (Series):

Ever & Always (Prequel)
Point Surrender
Cape Seduction
Angel's Gate

Alternative Romance Novella:

Starfire

www.ingramcontent.com/pod-product-compliance
Lightning Source LLC
Chambersburg PA
CBHW071146170626
46809CB00002B/794
* 9 7 8 0 6 9 2 2 0 8 2 6 7 *